GRAY DAWN

A Tropical Coast Thriller – Book 2

RILEY CURTS

ISBN 978-1-7771515-8-4 (paperback)/978-1-7781997-1-4 (large print)/ 978-1-7781997-0-7 (mobi)/ 978-1-7771515-9-1 (epub)

GRAY DAWN

PROLOGUE

"Cut him."

"Wait a minute, there's no need to be violent." The small wiry man glared up at the man who loomed over him.

Dark shadows slashed across the uneven floor. Candles burned in the far corner, casting a pale glow through the haze of dust motes. The dankness of rotting wood and mold permeated his nostrils, the pungent smell of rat shit and guano and human excrement teasing his gag reflex.

The big man's eyes narrowed as he squinted down at him in the murky darkness.

Bound to the chair, the wiry man stared back and struggled to keep an edge in his voice. He refused to be reduced to pleading. "You said you wouldn't hurt me."

"I say a lot of crap." The big man arched a brow and a sneer twisted his lip. He waved his hand dismissively and turned his attention to a third man who stood waiting, a blade glinting in his meaty hand, and repeated his earlier order. "Cut him."

"There's no reason for this," the wiry man yelled, writhing against the ropes that bound him, as the big man's lackey stepped toward him.

But he was talking to air and shadow.

As the cold hard steel of the knife pressed into the wiry man's cheek, the boss spoke again.

"Make sure there's lots of blood. We need lots of blood."

CHAPTER ONE

DAWN DEVON SAT ON THE AFT DECK OF THE PAPA JOE enjoying the afternoon sun. It had been a quiet day at the marina and she'd spent the first part of it puttering and setting up her new bistro table. It didn't take up a lot of room and had come with an umbrella to shelter her and her guest from the rays.

When she'd bought it, she'd stood in the aisle at the store arguing with herself about how impractical it was.

She'd have to dismantle it and take it down each time she took the boat out. It would only take five minutes to fold it up. Sure, but she didn't have space to stow it. And on it went.

After two minutes, she scooped the box up under her arm and hustled to the cashier before she could change her mind.

She was grateful for it now. Dawn pushed her empty plate to the side and raised her glass. "I'm glad you could make it, Megan."

Megan raised her glass and laughed. "Technically, I'm at a *client* meeting." She brushed her dark hair off her forehead and gazed out over the water. "Plus, I invited myself."

"I'm glad you did. I've been meaning to call you."

Megan waved her comment off. "Speaking of calling me, my friends call me Meg."

"Meg it is, then." Dawn raised her glass again.

Meg glanced around the back deck. "You must love living on this boat. It's so peaceful."

Dawn chuckled. "It's not always peaceful."

"I remember," Meg said, cocking her head to the side and surveying her more closely. "Your face is healing well."

"It wasn't the worst beating I've received."

Meg set her glass down on the small table. "You were pretty smashed up the last time I saw you."

"I remember," Dawn said, echoing Meg's earlier words. It had been outside the hotel at the south end of the marina, following a series of interviews with the Coast Guard. They'd promised to get together. Dawn had thought of Meg several times but hadn't followed up. "You didn't look so good yourself, if I recall."

Meg shrugged. "I was shaky for a couple of days, and… "

"What is it?" Dawn leaned forward.

"I have nightmares sometimes. Even when I'm awake. Them kicking Timothy or torturing Jenny. It plays on a loop in my mind." Her eyes dropped to the table and she refused to meet Dawn's gaze.

"It's normal. But it's behind us." She didn't want to revisit this. This afternoon was supposed to be about getting away from all of the memories that had haunted her for the last few weeks. Hell, for the last few years. She stood and gathered the plates. "Let's talk about something else."

"You think I'm weak," Meg said.

Dawn placed the plates back on the table. "Not at all. The truth is, it haunts me too. I was just hoping we could have some relief from all of that for a few hours."

Meg eyes misted and she stood. "I think that's a good idea. Let me help."

Dawn waved her back down. "It's two plates. Pour us more wine. I'll be right back." Stepping into the galley, she dropped the plastic plates into the trash. Jenny falling overboard flashed through her mind. An image of Joe falling overboard quickly followed. She shook her head and shoved her feelings back into her gut.

On the table in the galley, her phone rang. She checked the screen. An incoming call from Timothy.

Nope. That would totally ruin her day.

———

"I see you replaced the window in the front," Meg said.

"It wasn't really optional," Dawn said, again cursing the Cuban who had put a bullet through the wheelhouse window. Better the window than Meg, though.

"Insurance cover that?"

"For the most part." This girl was like a dog with a bone. Dawn tried to steer the conversation in another direction. "What else have you been doing aside from work?"

Meg caught her up on a family reunion weekend and a new guy she'd met speed dating. "You should try it."

Dawn shook her head. "Not for me," she said. "I have my hands full right here. There's still lots to do. Plus, I've been looking into getting my charter boat captain's license. I should be able to qualify in the next month or so."

"That's great," Meg said. She leaned forward conspiratorially. "I called Captain Birch."

"You called him?" Dawn tilted her head. "To go out?"

"Hell no," Meg said. "Remember what he said about us training for the Coast Guard?"

"Get out. You'd leave your job to do that?"

"Now would be the time," she said. "I've already started training so I can meet the physical requirements. Just in case." She pierced Dawn with a look. "Do you think I'm crazy?"

"Not at all," Dawn said. "I think you'd succeed at anything you do."

"Really?"

"Of course. I'm sure you're great at what you do now, the financial consulting thing, but honestly, I have a hard time picturing you behind a desk."

Meg's face lit up. "I'm only researching it right now. But it's nice to have options. Captain Birch has been really helpful. He asks about you each time we talk. You made quite an impression."

In the galley, Dawn's phone rang again. She grumbled and pushed her chair back. "Excuse me." She retrieved her phone. Timothy's number again. Her neighbor Triple T was nothing if not persistent. Returning to Meg, she turned the ringer to silent and put the phone down on the table.

"Tell me what you're doing for work outs," Dawn said. "Maybe we can start training together."

"Sure, I... " Meg's voice trailed off as the phone vibrated and a photo flashed on the screen. She leaned forward and her forehead creased with concern.

"Dawn," she said, her voice shaking as she pushed the cell toward Dawn. "Isn't that Timothy?"

CHAPTER TWO

Dawn pulled the phone toward her. Timothy's face filled the screen. A large gash slashed his right cheek, blood streamed down his face. Her gut clenched and, for a moment, she thought she might throw up the lasagna Meg had brought for lunch.

The cell vibrated again and another text came in: *Answer your phone.*

"What the hell?" Meg's eyes darted between the phone and Dawn.

Dawn shook her head. "I don't know. But it doesn't look good." *Thank you Captain Obvious.* The phone rang. The number was blocked. She picked up her cell. "Yes?"

"Dawn Devon?"

"Who is this?"

"Take me off speaker phone."

"You're not on—"

The voice lowered an octave, the caller speaking slowly and enunciating each word. "Take me off speaker phone."

Dawn shut off the speaker and held the phone up to her ear.

The voice was more threatening than the bloody photo of Timothy. "Fine," she said. "Now tell me who this is."

"I'll do the talking, Ms. Devon. Your job, if you want to see your friend alive again, is to listen very carefully to what I have to say."

Timothy her friend? They'd barely spoken in the last month. "I'm listening."

"Mr. Talbert has some funds on his boat and you are going to bring them to us. When you do, you can take Mr. Talbert home."

"I see." She didn't see. How the hell had Timothy gathered any so-called funds? He claimed to be as broke as usual and was still bitter, blaming her for his lack of funds.

"You'll find the money—"

"Don't do it, Dawn." Timothy yelled in the background. A loud crack sounded.

"Don't hurt him." Dawn's hand gripped the phone. Across the table from her, Meg stood and braced herself against the back of her chair. Dawn had no answers for the questions in her eyes.

"That's what he said." The cruelness of the laughter that came over the line chilled Dawn, her skin rippling with goose-bumps under the hot afternoon sky. "*Mister* Talbert advises you'll find the money in the forward cabin, at the back of a small cabinet in the head. Ten thousand dollars. You're to bring it here. You have two hours."

Dawn ran through a short list of people she could call for help. It didn't take her long. It was a very short list.

"And Ms. Devon?"

"Yes?"

"No police. Not if you want to see Talbert alive again."

"Wait. You said bring it here. Where is here?"

"We'll text you the coordinates. Keep your phone charged and with you at all times."

Dawn exhaled loudly as the caller hung up. Dropping the offending cell onto the table, she shook out her hand, her fingers cramped from her tight hold on the phone. Then her whole body started to shake.

CHAPTER THREE

"What is it?" Meg got right up in her face to get her attention and snapped her fingers two inches from her nose. "Dawn. What is it?"

Dawn focused on Meg. Her short list of people she could call for help included Timothy, and only Timothy. With him out of the picture, there was no one.

On the table, the phone vibrated and another photo of Timothy's bloody cheek filled the screen. Energy coursed through her and she sprang to her feet. "They've kidnapped Timothy."

"What? Who's they? Why would they call you?"

"I have no idea. But they want money from his boat." She picked up the phone and checked the time. "I have two hours."

"Two hours for what?"

"To get the money and go meet them."

"Meet them where?"

"Meg, I don't know." Dawn's words came out sharper than she intended. She put her palms up in the air. "Give me a minute. I'm still sorting it out myself. They're going to text me the location."

"How much money?"

"Ten grand."

"Timothy has ten thousand dollars stashed on his boat?"

Dawn paced across the deck, shaking her head. "I was thinking the same thing. I'm surprised to hear he has any money, let alone ten grand. Cripes, Meg, none of this makes sense. I mean, why *would* they call me?"

"Does Timothy have anybody else?"

"Not that I know of."

"You're physically the closest to his stash then. I don't know. He must have given them your number. Desperate people do desperate things."

"Or he didn't," Dawn said, pausing in place. "They might have gone through his phone. It's possible they don't even know that I'm at the marina. I could be a random contact they picked out of his phone."

Meg clicked her tongue. "I suppose. Seems unlikely though."

"It doesn't matter. I need to go. Keep an eye on that phone."

Dawn jumped down onto the pier and crossed to Timothy's boat, three slips down across from the Papa Joe. Standing at the stern, she sucked in a breath. She'd never been aboard. It felt intrusive. She climbed up and found the aft door unlocked. As she made her way forward, she took in her surroundings. Based on Timothy's usual rumpled appearance, she expected his boat would be a reflection of the man. But the interior cabins were neat, everything orderly and spotless.

In the small head, there were two cabinet doors. She came up empty on the first one. To reach the one in the corner by the toilet, she crouched on one knee, her elbow wedged against the plastic bowl as her fingers traced the two shelves, and the sides of the small space. Nothing. Huffing, she turned her arm and groped along the underside of the shelves feeling for a large envelope of cash. How large an envelope would he need for ten thousand dollars?

Her fingertips brushed something hard and cool to the touch. Heart pounding, she gripped the object and pulled it from its hiding place, the tape ripping away from the wood as she brought the weapon out into the light of day.

Dawn stared down at the gun in her hand. White heat snaked through her belly. There was no money. Timothy was sending her a message. The men who had him were dangerous. She'd figured that out on her own. How would finding his gun help her come up with ten thousand dollars?

Hoping there was something else, she did another careful search of the cabinet, but came up empty-handed. To be sure, she checked the first cabinet again. Nothing. The only thing was the weapon. Perched in the small space, her mind raced.

Timothy didn't have ten grand. How was she going to come up with that kind of money? Then it hit her. Mrs. Howe, the wealthy woman who had been on the failed cruising course, had given her a check. Dawn hadn't even opened it, determined not to cash it. One thing she couldn't deal with were handouts.

Mrs. Howe's words came back to her. The woman had insisted it was a gift, one she could easily afford. If Dawn wanted to keep Timothy safe, she'd have to push her pride to the side and take that check to the bank.

On her way off Timothy's boat, she spied a large stack of overdue bills on the back of his chart table. Ten grand cash hidden onboard. As if.

CHAPTER FOUR

Jumping off Timothy's boat, Dawn almost collided with Meg as she barreled toward her.

"Your phone keeps buzzing. I couldn't wait any longer." Meg's face fell as she met Dawn's eye. "Nothing?"

How much should she tell Meg? Aside from the cruising course, and a couple of quick texts to organize lunch, she barely knew the woman. Yet, here she was in the thick of things. She'd certainly come through the last time, Dawn knew she had a cool head and could be counted on. For the moment, she decided, she'd keep the discovery of the gun to herself. "No cash. As I suspected. What did they say?"

Meg extended her hand. "I didn't want to look. It's your phone."

Flicking the screen, Dawn scrolled through the notifications. She bit her lip as she scrolled past another photograph of Timothy's bloodied face. "They're getting impatient. I'm going to the bank."

Meg's eyebrows shot up. "You're going to front the ten grand?"

"What choice do I have? I can't leave him out there on his own." She hurried back to the Papa Joe with Meg on her heels.

Dawn rifled through a pile of unpaid bills and mail she'd pushed to the back of the galley table.

"Is there anything I can do?" Meg asked.

"I don't know yet." Dawn pulled the linen envelope from the stack of mail, slid her finger under the flap, and pulled the check out. Her breath hitched in her throat as she stared at the figure.

"Are you all right?"

"Yeah." Dawn shoved the check in a small backpack, checked that her wallet was inside, and met Meg's eye. "Can you stay?"

"Better," Meg said. "I can come with you."

"No, I think it's best if there's someone on board here. We don't know where these guys are. Can you stay?"

"Of course. Whatever you need."

Dawn slung the bag over her shoulder and shoved her cell in the back pocket of her cargo shorts. "I'll be back as fast as I can." She headed out then turned back and pulled the phone from her pocket. "Remember how to read a chart?"

Meg nodded. "Sure."

"This is the location they sent." Dawn scratched the numbers onto the back of an envelope and passed it to Meg. "Pinpoint where that is so I can go as soon as I get back."

"So *we* can go."

"I can't ask you to do that," Dawn said.

"You didn't ask, I offered."

There was no way she was exposing Meg to that kind of risk. But right now, she didn't have time for a debate. "Let's talk when I get back." Dawn spun away, leapt off the boat, and jogged up the pier.

As she reached the parking lot, Jeff, one of the marina

employees, flagged her down from the door of the marina store. Pretending to misunderstand, she smiled and raised her arm in an arc of a wave, then high-tailed it up to the street.

CHAPTER FIVE

The teller in the Merritt National Bank barely glanced at the check, all the zeros not holding the same shocking appeal as they had for Dawn. She pushed a strand of bleached blonde hair behind her ear and stifled a yawn as she initialed Dawn's deposit slip. "There will be a hold on this for ten business days."

Dawn gripped the edge of the counter. Behind her, a long line of customers waited to see one of the only two tellers working. "I need those funds today."

"It's standard banking policy," the young woman said. She consulted a calendar. "The funds will be released into your account on—"

"You don't understand," Dawn said, keeping her voice low. "I need at least some of that money today. How much can I withdraw today?"

"That's not really how it works. We have to wait for the full amount to clear."

"I need at least ten thousand dollars today. Today," she repeated, for good measure.

The girl leveled a look at her. "It's bank policy, ma'am."

Oh no. You don't ma'am me. Dawn's eyes dropped to the girl's name tag. "Cindi, I'll speak with your manager, please."

"Oh." Her head swiveled toward a closed office door to the right behind a long, side counter. "She's busy right now. But I assure you—"

"Have her come out," Dawn said. "I'll wait here."

"Ma'am—"

"Don't ma'am me, Cindi. My name is Dawn, or Ms. Devon, it's clearly marked on the deposit slip, the check and my account information you have open on your monitor."

The girl's eyes flared and her face paled. Dawn felt a small sense of satisfaction and progress. "Ms. Devon, I'll be happy to get the manager for you." She forced a smile that bared her small, white teeth. "Perhaps you could step to the side so we can serve some of our other customers? It may be a bit of a wait."

Dawn crossed her arms on the counter and leaned in. "I think I'll wait right here, Cindi." She winked at her and the girl flounced off. Dawn's heart pounded in her chest as the girl approached the other teller. They huddled together, whispering, casting worried glances in her direction. After a few seconds, the other teller returned her attention to the customer in front of her while Cindi waited dutifully behind. When the customer had completed his transaction, the senior teller stepped away and tapped on the manager's door.

Behind Dawn, a line of customers grew more restless, shuffling and griping among themselves. One woman in the front did so quite loudly. Dawn ignored her.

Moments later, the two tellers returned to their posts.

"The manager will see you now," Cindi said, turning on her heel. Dawn followed her to the end of the counter then stepped through a small gate. Cindi introduced Dawn before walking away.

The manager, a stick thin woman in a severely cut navy suit, stood behind her desk. "Ms. Devon," she said, voice smooth as silk. "Please come in and take a seat. I understand there's a problem with the check you're depositing today." Her eyes glanced down at the deposit slip and check on the blotter in front of her.

Dawn settled into one of the chairs. "Not a problem," she said. "I just wasn't expecting there to be a hold on the funds."

"It's standard," the woman said. Her head tilted as she looked at the endorsement then her eyes flicked to the top right corner. "This check is dated several weeks ago."

"I haven't had time to get to the bank. Look, isn't there something you can do?" Dawn's leg jittered and she clasped her hands over her knee to force it still. "I have an emergency today."

"I do hope everything is all right," the woman said smoothly, projecting not an ounce of concern. "Unfortunately, there isn't. If it was a bank draft, we could simply release the funds."

"I don't need the full fifty thousand," Dawn said. "I only need ten."

The manager relaxed into her chair, lacing her fingers over her abdomen. "We can't release a portion of it. We could look at giving you a short-term line of credit, perhaps. Do you have a loan history with us?"

Dawn's patience snapped. "I don't need a loan. I need access to these funds. The funds in this check." She leaned over the desk and tapped the paper. "Surely there's something. Can't you call the other bank and ask if the funds are available?"

The woman quirked a thin brow, the line as severe as the cut of her jacket. Her pale lips pursed in disapproval. "What I can suggest, Ms. Devon," she said, as she picked up the check and extended her arm across the desk, "is that you go in person to the other bank. They can verify the funds and possibly even cash it for you. Failing that, you can pay to have it certified and bring it back here to deposit."

Dawn snatched the paper from her and looked at the address. It was across town. She rose. "Do you know what time they close?"

"I'm sure you'll have time," the manager said, unfolding her body from the chair and extending her hand.

Not caring if the woman thought her rude, Dawn pivoted and sprinted through the bank, past the line of customers, past the security guard, and out the door. As the door closed behind her, the cell in her pocket started to vibrate.

CHAPTER SIX

THE SUN BOUNCED OFF THE SCREEN OF DAWN'S PHONE, making it impossible to see the message. She scuttled into a shadow of a nearby pillar and opened the text. Timothy's face, his left eye blood-shot, the lid swollen and purple. Her finger twitched to respond.

A second text came in: *Giddy up, cowgirl.*

Dawn stared at the offending message then jammed the phone back in her pocket and took off down the stairs, scanning the street for a free taxi.

A newish black sedan with tinted windows pulled up to the curb where she stood. Annoyed, she moved toward the back of the car so she could flag down an approaching cab.

The car backed up and the passenger window slid down. A man called her name. The muscles in her back tightened. Her instincts screamed at her to run. She waved frantically at the cab in the outside lane.

"Dawn, it's Wayne."

Wayne? She leaned down. Captain Wayne Cutter, Joe's old friend from the Coast Guard, stretched across the front seat of the car. He was dressed in civilian clothes. "Hi, Wayne."

"I spotted you coming down the stairs and haven't seen you in a bit. How are things?"

Dawn shifted her weight, the phone pressing against her backside as she leaned down to the window. An unwelcome reminder. She didn't have time for this.

"Great," she lied. "Sorry Wayne, I'm in a bit of a time crunch at the moment. Can we catch up later?"

"Where you headed? I'll give you a lift." He smiled broadly, his kind eyes fixed on her.

She glanced up the street. Not a single taxi in sight. "I'm going across town."

One eyebrow arched but he smiled again and said, "No problem. Jump in, I'll get you there." He pushed open the door. With no other option, she slid into the passenger seat and he pulled into traffic.

"It's been, what, a month?"

"Yes. I should thank you again for helping out with that." She paused, trying to frame the next question. "How is that investigation going? You mentioned other agencies were involved."

"I probably shouldn't have," he said, his fingers drumming a beat on the wheel. "There's nothing new to report but I've heard they're making some progress."

"Which means?"

"Sorry, I can't share more than that right now but I'll keep you in the loop when we have something concrete."

Dawn watched the people crossing in front of them at the red light.

He glanced sidelong at her. "You know, Joe and I went way back. I want you to know that if you need anything - on the water or off - you can consider me a friend."

"That's very kind," she said. Emotional displays made her uncomfortable and she wished she'd waited for a taxi. Not that she had the luxury to wait for anything at the moment.

Wayne guided the car expertly through the afternoon traffic. "You have a time constraint, you said?"

"I'm trying to reach the bank before it closes." She itched to tell him why and enlist his help. They'd warned her about involving the authorities. Would Wayne be able to help her as a friend and keep the authorities out of it? The smart move was to risk it.

Wayne pulled his left arm up from the wheel and his cuff slid back to display a Cartier watch, very similar to the one Joe used to wear. She'd seen the same watch on Thomas Duncan's wrist when he'd read her Joe's will. Dawn's words died on her lips.

"It's quarter past," Wayne said. "Should give you another forty-five minutes and I'll have you there in under five."

When Cutter pulled up to the curb, she thanked him and reached for the door. As she pushed it open, he grabbed her left arm. "I can wait and bring you back to the Marina."

"I can't ask you to do that," she said. Especially since she wasn't going straight back to the boat. She'd need to return to her bank first.

"It's no trouble. It's my day off. I'm a bit at loose ends, to be honest."

She looked into his eyes. She needed the drive. Anything that would hurry things along at this point would be helpful. "Okay. I won't be long."

"Sir, you can't park here." A traffic cop tapped on the roof of Cutter's car. Dawn took the opportunity to slide out, shutting the car door behind her.

"I'll only be a minute, officer," Wayne said.

The young officer shook his head. "Sorry, no stopping here."

"Dawn, I'll circle the block. Watch for me when you come out."

"Sure, thanks," she called and sprinted toward the stairs.

What was it about Cutter that he was always showing up when she needed him? Like her own personal guardian angel.

CHAPTER SEVEN

Dawn stood on the steps of Mrs. Howe's bank, her cell pressed to her ear, trying to drown out the ambient noise so she could hear clearly. A man with a large briefcase cursed at her and sidestepped to get past her.

"I'm already moving as fast as I can," Dawn said into the phone. "I had some complications."

"If you want to see Mr. Talbert alive again, it's time for you to *simplify* your *complications*. I want you on your way within the hour. Do you understand?"

"Yes."

"Say the words. Say you understand." The man's harsh tone assaulted her ears, his words clipped.

She bristled. "Fine. I understand." The line went dead.

Dawn scanned the street in front of the bank and swallowed hard. The traffic cop paced along the curb. Cutter's car was nowhere in sight.

Glancing at the screen of her phone, she did a quick calculation. She didn't have time to return to her bank if she needed to be back at the marina within the next hour. Her fingers clutched the strap of her small backpack. The idea of walking around with fifty thousand in cash made her want to throw up. But Timothy was running out of time. She had to choose. A human life or having her money securely locked up.

She shrugged the pack onto both shoulders, keeping it against her chest like a baby carrier and raced down the street toward the intersection to find a cab.

CHAPTER EIGHT

"Come on," Dawn hissed under her breath as the cab crawled through the afternoon traffic. In the last ten minutes, she'd wished ten times she'd waited for Cutter and his efficient way of skirting lane to lane.

"What's that, ma'am?" The driver glanced into his rearview, his heavy-lidded eyes piercing hers.

Again with the ma'am. She leaned forward, wrapped her fingers around the back of the seat. "I'm in a horrible hurry, sir."

"Not a terrible rush?" In the mirror, the driver waggled his bushy brows comically. *"We're in a terrible rush?"*

"What?" Dawn's question came out sharper than she intended. But she didn't care. She wasn't in the mood for games.

"It's a quote from *The Princess Bride*. When they take Cary Elwes in to see Miracle Max, and—"

"I really need you to get me to the marina as fast as possible."

He shrugged and dropped his gaze back to the road. "Your ride," he said. Then he mumbled something that sounded like people being in too big of a rush for everything these days.

Dawn ignored him and watched the buildings crawl by, her knee bouncing against the back of the seat.

Bailing out of the taxi the instant it hit the marina parking lot, Dawn dashed toward the dock. Out of the corner of her eye, she spied Jeff. Again, he raised an arm to detain her. She waved back and didn't miss a step as she hit the dock running. As she approached the Papa Joe, she slowed her gait, taking a moment to compose herself before seeing Meg.

But it wasn't Meg she saw on the stern of her boat. It was a broad back with squared shoulders, arms gesturing wildly. Had the kidnappers come to meet her? Worried, she picked up the pace. As she advanced, she heard Meg's laughter ring through the air. She sat across from the man, arms on her belly and tears streaming down her face. When she spotted Dawn, she stood, swiping at her eyes.

"Dawn, look who came by."

Erik stood and turned toward her, extending his hand to help her back onboard. "It's great to see you again, Dawn."

The Professor, as she dubbed him when they'd met. Dawn cocked her head. "And you, Erik. I haven't seen you since the course."

"It's like a mini-reunion," Meg said.

Erik's eyes twinkled. "We were just laughing about that. I was telling Megan—I mean, Meg," he raised his brow as he caught Meg's eye, "one of the stories Mr. Howe told us when we were all off in the speed boat together that night. The man was actually very entertaining. Considering how nervous we were, his stories helped keep our minds off things."

Could Erik showing up here today, at this time, be a coincidence? There was something just outside of her grasp that she couldn't put her finger on. She struggled to nail the thought down, but it eluded her. More urgently, she needed to get rid of him as fast as possible and get on her way. Right after she stashed the backpack, now plastered to her chest from the afternoon heat. "Give me one minute," she said, holding up a finger.

In the galley, she lifted one of the bench seats and dropped the backpack in. So much money in one small grey bag. In her possession. On her boat. Her stomach flipped.

In her pocket, the phone buzzed. She glanced at the notification. An image of a ticking clock. The kidnappers had a sense of humor. Too bad she did not.

She needed to get rid of the Professor.

"Hey, Meg, give me a hand in here?"

When Meg came through the door, Dawn motioned her to follow her up into the wheelhouse. "Look, I need to go. Can you invite Erik for a drink or something and you guys take off?"

Meg's eyes narrowed. "I'm not letting you do this alone. I'm coming with you."

"No. Not under any circumstances," she said. "It's too risky."

"Dawn." Meg wrapped her hand around Dawn's upper arm and Dawn pulled away, she didn't have time for any of this. Meg planted her hands on her hips. "I'm coming with you," she said. "I think we should take Erik, too."

"Erik? Look, I'd be crazy to take you along, why would I involve someone else?"

"Come on. Erik's level-headed. We have no idea what we're walking into."

"No, *I* have no idea what I'm walking into."

"Geez, you're hard-headed."

Dawn felt a smile twitch at her lip. "Seriously? You think you know me well enough to say that?"

"Probably not." Meg's lips pursed. She stepped back a couple of inches and threw her palms up in the air. "Sorry."

"It's fine," Dawn said, regretting her words as hurt flickered across Meg's face. She relented. "I am hard-headed. I thought I hid it well."

Meg grinned and raised her brows. "You don't."

Dawn glanced out over the water. Whatever decision she made, she needed to make it quickly. Meg was right about one thing. She had no idea what she was walking into. Whatever it was, it would be more difficult alone.

"Fine," she said. "Come with me. Let's tell Erik what's going on." She moved away but Meg's hand shot out and grabbed her upper arm again.

"The ransom. Did you get it?"

"I did."

"All of it?"

Dawn thought of the stacks of bills in the small backpack. Of the fifty thousand dollars in cash stashed in the galley.

"Yep. Let's go talk to Erik."

CHAPTER NINE

"Based on the coordinates you gave me," Meg said, stabbing her finger at a small island, "this is where they want us to meet them."

Dawn, Meg, and Erik leaned over the chart table. "We're only a couple of hours away from there," Dawn said.

"Are you thinking we'll go in the Papa Joe?" Erik asked, tracing his finger along a course. "No disrespect, but your top speed would be what? Fourteen knots at best?"

"Timothy has a Boston whaler. We'll take that."

Her new friends stood across from her, shoulder to shoulder, the chart stretching before them on the table. They both looked nervous.

"Second thoughts? You don't have to come with me. I can go alone."

Erik and Meg shook their heads. "No," they said in unison.

"Let's get to it. You go on ahead and I'll lock up here. Meg, you know which boat is Timothy's?"

"Yes, but I don't know which speedboat."

"Right. Wait for me on the dock, I'll just be a minute."

Erik was gone before she'd finished her sentence. Her hand

shot out as Meg turned to leave. Meg turned back to her, her face open, a question in her eyes. Dawn wanted to say thank you. It had been a long time since she'd had someone she felt she could count on. Instead, she rolled the chart and passed it to Meg. "Take this with you."

Once she was alone on board, she grabbed the backpack she'd left in the galley and took it forward. She stacked ten grand on the shelf over the starboard bunk, then moved the mattress and bedding from the port bunk, lifted the board beneath and opened the metal security locker Joe had built. She dumped the rest of the money into the large locker. The stacks of bills looked lonely in that space.

With her luck the damn boat would blow up or someone would set it on fire and she'd never see the money again. Squashing her anxiety down, she closed the lid, snapped the combination lock, and put the mattress and bedding back in place.

She retrieved the ten grand and rolled it in a long sleeve shirt, stuffed it in the backpack, then hustled up the stairs.

Show time.

CHAPTER TEN

SQUINTING into the sun, DAWN huddled over the outboard engine on the back of Timothy's skiff.

"Do you think we flooded it?" Meg asked.

"Possibly," Erik said. The two of them hovered over Dawn's shoulder like boneless gargoyles.

"I don't smell gas, do you?" Dawn tilted her head as she spoke, hoping one of them had more ideas than she did.

Both Erik and Meg shook their heads. Erik had the decency to sniff the air first. "Want me to try?" he asked, gesturing toward the dead outboard.

Dawn shifted out of his way. "Please." Her chest had started to tighten. She was painfully aware of the time, the cell phone in her pocket felt like a ticking time bomb. Any second it could vibrate and ring again and each time it did, it set her nerves ablaze. If they couldn't figure out the problem soon, they'd have to come up with another plan. It felt like she'd only been awake a few hours and already the day had been jam-packed and fraught with obstacles. Her patience was running thin, a familiar thread of anger surging up inside her.

Beside her, Meg watched her intently. "How you holding up?"

"Fine." Dawn wanted to punch a wall but best to keep those thoughts to herself. "You?"

Meg raised her brows and her mouth twisted to the side. "Oh-kay."

"You see anything, Erik?" Dawn shifted her weight from one foot to the other, the small boat rocking as she moved.

"Not really. It's possible it's not getting enough gas. Let's try again."

Dawn stepped back to the ignition, turned it. Again nothing.

"Is there a manual override?" Meg asked.

"There should be," Erik said. Dawn was already going through the controls. He stepped up beside her, his shoulder brushing hers. She edged to the side. "Here," he said, flicking a switch. "Let me try again."

He moved back to the engine and pulled the draw cord on the big 150 horse power Mercury. It was enough engine to propel the little boat over the waves more than twice as fast as Dawn's. But again, nothing.

Erik rolled back on his haunches, his long arms resting on his knees. "I'm out of ideas."

"Let me take one more look." She climbed down onto the swimming platform and knelt beside the motor. She ran her fingers along the gas line, climbed back up and followed it along the underside of the gunwale. Mid-way to the wheel, her fingers brushed over something jagged. Lowering herself to the deck, she craned her neck. She dug her cell phone from her back pocket and shined the light on the thin clear tubing. "This gas line has been cut."

"Let's see." Erik dropped to the deck beside her. "Huh."

Meg also knelt down on the other side of Dawn. "Maybe it

broke? Worn through?" She peered at the spot Dawn had the light on. "Oh. That line looks brand new and the cut is clean."

"What the hell does this mean?" Erik said. He raised his head and his skull thunked as he cracked it into the gunwale.

"Careful," Meg said.

Dawn took a breath, the anxiety in her gut inching uncomfortably up through her chest. "I don't know. Aside from the fact that we'll now have to go in my boat." She stood and brushed her knees off.

Meg planted herself in front of Dawn, hands clasped. "Do you think someone sabotaged Timothy's boat?"

"You make it sound like it's a big conspiracy. It could be—"

"Coincidence?" Meg uttered a small laugh. "I think we can start to assume there's more going on here than we know."

"There's time for both of you to back out and I wouldn't blame you a bit." She folded her arms and fixed them both with a stare. "But in or out, I need to get going."

CHAPTER ELEVEN

In the wheelhouse of the Papa Joe, Dawn turned the ignition key to check the fuel gauge. Half full. Or was it half empty? Either way, she had enough gas to get out there but barely enough to make it back.

"We need to fuel up before we go," she said. "Erik, can you cast off the bow? Meg, you take the stern." She fired up the engine and once Erik and Meg were back on board, idled over to the pumps at the far end of the next pier.

Erik and Meg jumped off with lines and secured the boat.

Grabbing her gas card from the galley cabinet, Dawn hopped down beside the pump. She set up the nozzle and swiped her card to begin. Nothing happened. She swiped the card a second time. Again nothing. Cursing under her breath, she checked everything one more time and tried again. "Damn it." She slapped her hand against the side of the pump.

"What's the problem, want me to look?" Erik hovered at her side. He slid into the space beside her, pushed her gently out of the way and meticulously went through the steps she'd just taken.

She snorted in frustration. "It's not working. There must be something wrong with the card reader."

"What can I do?" asked Meg.

"Can you run up to the office and find Jeff?"

"Sure. Where will I find him?"

"When you hit the parking lot, look to your two o'clock. There's a door that says Store. Once you're inside, go past the store, and he has a little office two doors down on the left. You can't miss it."

"Be right back," Meg said over her shoulder as she hurried away.

The Professor continued to jiggle the buttons and slide her card through the slot. "What do you think the problem is?"

"Beats me," Dawn said. "'Cause it's Tuesday?"

Erik raised his brows in silent question.

She shrugged. "Seems I'm thwarted at every step today. There doesn't seem a plausible explanation for most of it, so why not blame it on Tuesday?"

Resting his arm across the top of the pump, Erik laughed. "I've had my own issues with Tuesday. Mostly in the past though."

Dawn took a breath and tried to return his smile. "I'm worried."

"I know. A lame attempt to lighten the mood."

She looked out over the water. "I have no idea what we're going to face out there."

Erik sighed. "Let's take it one step at a time. For now, we focus on getting gas."

"Right. Of course. Tell me, how is your sabbatical going?"

"Really?"

She shrugged. "Why not? I'm going in circles otherwise."

He tipped his head, shielded his eyes from the glare of the sun bouncing off the water. "It's going well. I love the weather here, for one thing."

"Dawn." Meg ran down the dock toward them, waving a sheet of paper. She stopped short of them, out of breath, and shoved the paper toward Dawn. "Jeff's not there. This was on his door."

Please note that effective immediately, the chip reader on the gas pumps ...

"Oh crap," Dawn said. Her eyes ran quickly over the rest of the note. "That's why," she said, understanding why Jeff had been so anxious to flag her down the last couple of times she'd seen him. When would she learn avoidance never worked for her? At the bottom of the page, his work cell was listed. She pulled out her phone and dialed.

"Jeff, it's Dawn. Are you out for lunch?"

"Appointment," he said. "And hello to you, too."

"Sorry." She bit her tongue. "I need gas. When will you be back?"

"About forty-five minutes, I guess."

"Is there someone else?"

"Someone else what?"

"That can give me my new gas card."

"Oh, that. No. You didn't see any of the signs we had posted? There's one at the store, at the laundry, in the showers, by the lockers, on the bulletin board—"

"Jeff, I didn't see the signs. That doesn't matter now. Can you come to the pumps as soon as you get back?"

"You betcha." And with that he was gone. She flicked her screen.

"Forty-five minutes," she said, addressing Erik and Meg. She paced across the small space. "It's been almost an hour since they told me to get underway within the hour."

"It's not like they can see us," Meg said.

"We don't know that for sure," Erik said, glancing from Meg to Dawn. "They must be keeping tabs on you somehow."

"I think so, too," she said. She paced, her mind racing. "Wait. Maybe Timothy has his new card."

"Doesn't it need a PIN or something?" Meg asked.

"Yes, but it's worth a shot. I don't know what else to do."

"Okay, should I go?"

"Why don't you both go?" Dawn said. "Two looking will be more efficient. I'll stay here. Maybe someone else will come along with a working card."

"Right." Erik nodded and he and Meg walked off toward the parking lot and the other dock.

Dawn checked the time. Her hour was almost up. If Erik was right and they were somehow watching her, they'd be calling any minute.

CHAPTER TWELVE

Standing on the open dock with the bright sun beating down on her head, Dawn felt exposed. She clambered back onto the Papa Joe and sat in a slice of shadow against the galley cabin keeping an eye on the dock. At this time of day, someone else should come along needing gas. Surely someone would want to go out for the sunset. Across the harbor in the more upscale marina, the one filled with better boats and deeper pockets, a steady stream of boats poured out of the channel.

She supposed most of her neighbors weren't home from work yet. The curse of being a live-aboard in a primarily live-aboard marina. A working stiff among other blue collars or layabouts. She pondered for a moment which category she might fit into. When it came right down to it, she didn't much care as long as she had a roof over her head.

Taking the phone from her pocket, she laid it on the deck beside her, watching the time and working backwards. She'd been in the car with Cutter at two fifteen. Out of the bank and on her way back before three. She'd looked over the charts with Meg and Erik, messed about with Timothy's outboard, gone over to the pumps for gas. Why had she not noted the time the last time they called her.

Then it struck her. She'd been so focused on solving the problem she'd missed the obvious. She opened her phone and checked recent calls. It was slightly over an hour since they'd called. How could she persuade them to back off and leave Timothy alone until they could get there? Wait, what if they wanted her to come alone? They hadn't said that. She'd be careful with her language. Careful to use I, not we.

She placed the phone down beside her and watched for Jeff. It had been almost twenty minutes. If there was a god, his appointment would wrap up early or Erik and Meg would find Timothy's gas card. Of course, even with the card she'd have to try and figure out his PIN. She barely knew the man, so unless it was 1234 her chances were slim to none.

The little guy with the pick axe chipped against her belly. Fifty thousand dollars. She'd almost choked when she'd seen the amount on Mrs. Howe's check. It made her feel hugely indebted. How could it not? The woman had said there were no strings attached, but in Dawn's experience, nobody gave anyone something for nothing. She'd never intended to cash it. Hell, she'd never intended to even open it. It was a nice gesture and it should have been left at that.

Fifty thousand dollars. Even after paying the ransom, she'd have forty thousand bucks. It couldn't come at a better time. She was still flat broke and busted. Her life a country and western song. She didn't even have a dog or a truck. That would have been a step up.

Dawn bolted to a standing position. What was she thinking? Her life was already a mess and it was one thing to endanger herself. But to expose Meg and Erik to that kind of trouble? She shook her head. She couldn't do it. Whoever had Timothy had already hurt him. Might even kill him. Bile inched up her throat. She choked.

If she went out there, with Meg and Erik, she'd be putting two more lives in danger. After the death and loss she'd experienced recently, she couldn't afford to take that chance.

She wouldn't take that chance. She would call the police. When Meg and Erik got back, she'd let them know. Crisis averted.

At the end of the pier, she spotted Jeff pull into the lot in his battered pickup. She drew a deep breath into her lungs and let it out slowly. Jeff disappeared into the building and five minutes later made his way down the dock toward her. She jumped down beside the pump to greet him.

"Here it is," he said, extending the plastic card. "We installed a new scanner so everyone had to get a new card."

She nodded. "You explained that on the phone."

"Yeah, well." He shoved his hands in his pockets. "What's the big emergency? Urgent sunset calling your name?" he asked peevishly.

Dawn reached out and touched his upper arm. "Thanks, Jeff. I appreciate you rushing back for this." She didn't need gas now. But she could make a show of it. Put something in the tank, at least. She swiped the card and her finger hovered over the keypad. "Same PIN as before?"

"Yep." Jeff slanted his gaze discreetly to the other side of the pier as she jabbed in her PIN. When Dawn lifted the nozzle he stepped over and took it from her. "Let me take care of that."

"Really, Jeff, I do appreciate you rushing back to help with this."

"I know," he said, a smile tugging at his lip. He lowered his head, a blush creeping up his cheeks. Oh, no. Was it possible Jeff had a thing for her? That would be awkward.

Her phone trilled and she stepped away, putting her back to him as he pumped the diesel.

"Ms. Devon," came the voice she now knew and hated.

"I'm here."

"I see that. Why are you not on your way *here*?"

Dawn turned in a full circle. He could see her? He could be almost anywhere. On one of the boats nearby. In the Marina Marriott Hotel. Or on one of the boats dotting the harbor. "I needed gas," she said. "I'm filling up now."

"This is not a leisurely pleasure trip, Ms. Devon. Don't get confused about that." In the background, she heard Timothy grunt in pain.

"Leave him alone. I said I'll be there."

"Ms. Devon, if you don't come, I will kill Mr. Talbert. If you call the police, I will kill Mr. Talbert. And then, I will come and kill you."

Dawn's hand trembled as she clenched the phone.

"Say you understand, Ms. Devon."

"I understand," she said, her teeth gritted. "Don't kill him. Don't hurt him again."

The laugh that echoed through the line sounded evil to the core. "Ah, Ms. Devon, no need to get emotional. Do what you're told, and all will be right with your world. I'm going to hang up now, you're going to finish getting gas, and get under way. Immediately. Remember, it's not only Mr. Talbert's life on the line."

The line hissed with dead air. Dawn felt sucker punched.

CHAPTER THIRTEEN

"All done here." Jeff slid the nozzle back into the pump and wiped his hands off on a rag that hung by the pump.

"Thanks, Jeff. Mind casting me off?"

"No problem."

Dawn hopped on board, taking the stern line with her. She checked the parking lot and the end of the other pier. Still no sign of Erik and Meg. If she couldn't abort, if she couldn't call the cops, at least she could leave them behind and out of danger.

She started the diesel and Jeff walked alongside as she idled up along the dock toward the end.

"Dawn!"

Damn, it was Meg.

"Toss the line, Jeff," she yelled down.

Jeff stood on the pier, eyes shifting from Dawn to Erik and Meg pounding down the dock toward him.

"Wait," Erik yelled to Jeff. Jeff wrapped his hand tightly around the bow line and held it in place.

Dawn continued to idle forward. There was still a chance she'd get away. "Push me off, Jeff."

Jeff threw his hands up. "Someone is coming. It sounds urgent."

Behind her, there was a loud thump as Erik jumped onto the stern. "Slow down, Dawn," he yelled.

On the dock, Jeff's mouth dropped open. "What the hell? Are these friends of yours? Slow down, Dawn."

Dawn shifted the engine into neutral, the big boat continued to drift forward. When Jeff reached the end of the pier, he let loose a string of disgusted curses, and threw the bowline up to the deck.

She heard Erik helping Meg. "Take my hand." Then they were both onboard and crashing through the galley toward her. She pushed the throttle forward and headed for the buoy, leaving Jeff standing on the pier shaking his head after her.

CHAPTER FOURTEEN

Erik bolted into the wheelhouse, face reddened and his eyes stormy. "What the hell, Dawn?"

Behind him, Meg's brow furrowed as she stared at Dawn. "What happened? Your face is ash white."

Erik flicked his wrist, dismissing Meg's question. "Never mind that, why did you try to take off without us?"

Dawn kept her eyes on the buoy and small craft in front of her. "You shouldn't be here. It's too dangerous."

"Something else happened," Meg pressed. "Tell us what."

Dawn clenched the wheel and tried to calm herself. "The less you know the better. I shouldn't have told you about this at all."

Erik got up in her face. "Is that why you sent us on that wild goose chase? Trying to find Timothy's gas card?"

She turned toward him, frustrated. "No, I sent you because we needed gas." Erik glared at her. "It's true," she added.

"I'm not sure what to believe right now." Erik widened his stance and crossed his arms in front of his chest.

Dawn recognized the defiance in Erik's stance. She needed these people. Short of turning back and forcing them off the boat, they were here now. The fight drained out of her and fear crept back in. "Fine." She glanced over to Meg. "When Jeff was finishing up with the gas, they called and told me to leave immediately. I also thought I could keep you out of danger if I left you behind."

"And go out there alone?" Meg's voice was shrill. "What else? They said something to shake you. Did they send more photos? Is Timothy okay?"

"Only more threats and bullying," Dawn lied. "Status quo. But they're watching, I think, and they're running out of patience." She needed time to think, to process. "Look, I am glad you're here. Why don't we get some food in us? Hard to say when we'll have another chance to eat."

"Sure," Meg said, her lips pursed. "I'll see what I can put together."

Erik looked at Dawn. She avoided his eyes and fixed hers on the horizon. "I'll help," he said and turned away.

———

Dawn braced herself behind the wheel of the Papa Joe and shook out her hands, willing the tightness to drain through her fingers. Then she rested them lightly on the smooth, worn wood of the wheel, and let the vibration of the diesel beneath her feet soothe her rattled nerves. Sunlight bounced off the turquoise surface of the water as she navigated past the buoy at the mouth of the harbor and into the open channel.

In the galley, Meg and Erik talked quietly, preparing a light meal from the food she and Meg had left over from lunch. Dawn had no idea what she was walking into, and the weight of having Erik and Meg on board, putting them in danger, weighed heavily on her. At the same time, she was glad she didn't have to face it alone. She tried to rationalize away her guilt. They were both adults and could make their own decisions. During the disastrous cruising course, they'd already proven they could handle themselves under pressure.

None of that made a pinch of difference. She was responsible for them now and they were sailing straight into the path of serious danger. She had zero doubt Timothy's kidnappers would come for her and kill her if she didn't show up with the ransom. A few months ago - certainly in the time before she met Joe - she would have been happy to have someone put a bullet in her head. Put her out of her misery. Now she was rebuilding her life, making connections with people, and, for the first time in years, life actually felt worth living.

Besides, things could also go smoothly. She could show up, pay the ransom, gather Timothy and even be back at the marina in time for a late supper. It could happen.

"Olives?" Meg yelled up.

"In what?"

"Never mind," Erik said, poking his head through the door. His hair fell over his eyes and, for the first time, she noticed how boyish his face was. "We'll just bring you a plate."

She nodded, happy not to have more decisions to make, and kept her eye on the horizon. Who would have kidnapped Timothy? And how would they know she had money? Dawn replayed the day the wealthy woman from the cruising course, Mrs. Howe, and her lawyer had turned up to give her the check. The three of them had been standing on the dock, directly beside the Papa Joe. She remembered being aware of keeping her voice down even though there hadn't been anyone else around.

Timothy had not been anywhere in sight. Was it possible he knew Mrs. Howe had given her money? Had he been on his boat eavesdropping on their conversation? She tried to imagine how far their voices would have carried. She didn't think he would hear the exact exchange. But he might have seen the lawyer give her the envelope. He might have put the pieces together on his own.

Her relationship with Timothy had always been difficult, and he hadn't forgiven her for refunding the cruising course fees, but she didn't think he'd stoop to this. Faking his own kidnapping? Forcing her into danger so he could extort money?

She shook her head. Given the extent of his injuries and the tone of the caller, it didn't seem plausible. Her paranoia was getting the better of her.

But if Timothy hadn't set her up, why call her to pay his ransom? Who would have cut his gas line? And why? She scoured her memory. Had there been someone on the docks the last few days? Someone who didn't belong there? She didn't think so. Although it could have happened while she was away, or asleep, or just not paying attention. Most of the time, the marina felt like a safe haven and vigilance wasn't part of her normal routine.

She had more questions than answers. None of it made sense to her.

CHAPTER FIFTEEN

Erik waved a plate under Dawn's nose. "Hungry?"

"I'm not sure I can eat."

He shrugged and put the plate down on the chart table. "Eating was your idea."

"Did you find anything on Timothy's boat?"

He leaned his back against the chart table, his eyes narrowed. "We didn't find his gas card, if that's what you mean."

"Anything else?"

"You asked us to poke around to find the card."

"Erik, it's important. Did you see anything else that might, I don't know, throw some light on his kidnapping?" She glared at him, frustrated at his stubbornness. "You're going to have to get over being annoyed with me for trying to leave you behind. I already told you why I did it."

He rolled his eyes and looked past her shoulder to the island they were cruising past. "Well... I'm no Sherlock but I noticed a large stack of overdue bills on the table, so clearly he's either lazy or short on funds."

"I noticed those, too. Anything else?"

"Did you see his calendar?"

"Like a wall calendar?" Dawn said.

"No, he had a small agenda that was open on the galley counter next to the stove."

"What did it say?"

"Well, Watson, it had something written on today's date with a red circle around it."

"What?"

"I couldn't make it out. His writing is messy. It looked like some kind of shorthand. It was only a few letters."

"Do you remember what exactly?"

"I don't. We were rushing to try to find the card. It might come back to me later."

"Was there a time? A location? Anything?"

Erik tilted his head. "No. Nothing like that. But I did notice a small bag already packed on one of the front bunks."

"What kind of bag?"

"A small gray duffel."

"Sounds like Timothy's go bag. I think he keeps that ready for last-minute charter jobs."

"Maybe," Erik said. "Correct me if I'm wrong but I didn't get the impression that you and Timothy have a great relationship. Things seemed pretty confrontational between you when we first met."

"We're not besties, that's for sure." Dawn shrugged and glanced over at her plate.

Erik tracked her eyes and stepped toward the wheel. "Why don't you go ahead and eat with Meg and I'll take over here?"

Dawn pointed out their course, relinquished the wheel and retrieved her plate.

Meg came into the wheelhouse and sat on the bench. Dawn sat beside her, picking at the plate of cheese, crackers, cold cuts and olives.

"How long until we get to the rendezvous point?" Meg knew the answer already, but Dawn recognized the question for what it was. Nerves. Meg seeking to somehow make sense of it all.

"At least another hour and a half," Dawn said, popping an olive into her mouth. She savored the salty burst on her tongue.

"We haven't heard from them in a while. Why do you think that is?" Meg's forehead furrowed.

Dawn paused and put her fork down on the plate in her lap. "I don't know but let's enjoy the reprieve."

"You said you thought they might be watching us."

Erik turned from his post. "Right. How would they be watching us?"

Dawn set her plate on the bench and stood, pacing from one side to the other. "How could they be watching us?"

"Maybe they had someone posted near the marina," Meg offered.

"Possibly." Dawn replayed her arrival back at the marina. Jumping out of the taxi, rushing down the dock. She remembered Jeff waving to her but she'd paid no attention to the cars in the lot or who else had been around. She hadn't noticed anything out of place, but then, she hadn't been looking for anything either. "I don't know."

"Maybe they're just giving us time to get there. We can't be certain they're watching," Erik said.

"Yeah, well, just because we're paranoid doesn't mean they're not after us." Dawn braced herself against the open starboard door and scanned the horizon.

"What?" Meg asked.

She glanced back over her shoulder. "Old joke. They might have had someone posted or not. Our goal remains the same. Get to our meet point and bring Timothy home in one piece." She pulled her cell from her pocket and checked the signal. Three bars. Any calls would come through. She stalked to the chart table, tossed the phone down and checked their position before returning to the bench. She sat and cleared off her plate.

Meg watched her, picking at the food on her own plate.

"Eat up," Dawn said, jutting her chin toward Meg's food. It could turn into a very long day and having something in her belly might interrupt the hamster wheel of crazies that were gnawing at Dawn's insides. At least, that was her hope.

CHAPTER SIXTEEN

THE PHONE RANG. IT SAT ON THE CHART TABLE WHERE DAWN had left it, ringing and vibrating its way across the open chart. She sprang from her place on the bench.

"Speak of the devil," Erik said.

Dawn opened the call. "Yes?"

"Give me your location." As usual, the caller's voice was clipped and curt. The very sound of it made her blood boil.

Dawn relayed their position.

"You're making good time in that old tub."

Dawn bristled. His tone rubbed her the wrong way. Was he actually making light of the situation? And insulting her boat? "We'll be there shortly."

"Hang on, Ms. Devon. Watch for a text from me. I'm sending you new coordinates."

The line went dead. She held the phone out, staring at the screen.

"What is it?" Meg asked.

"He's sending a new location." She stalked across the wheelhouse, trying to burn off her anxiety, eyes fixed to the screen.

Her phone pinged. She opened the text. It was another photograph of Timothy. The side of his face now so swollen one of his eyes was completely closed. His nose looked broken, skewed to the side. Dried blood caked under his nostrils, ringed his upper lip. Meg peered over her shoulder and gasped.

Dawn's phone pinged a second time. She opened the text and walked to the chart. "Here," she said, pinpointing the location. "He wants us to go the reef near Ghost Head Island."

The reef where she and Joe took Dylan and his pals diving. The reef where Joe went overboard. The reef where she last enjoyed a kind word and a laugh with her friend.

"Did he say why there's a new location?" Erik said.

Dawn huffed. "What do you think?"

Erik raised a brow and turned back to the wheel. Meg's nose crinkled and she shook her head at Dawn.

Crossing to the wheel, Dawn said, "I'm sorry. I'm stressed but it's no reason to take it out on you."

"Damn straight it's not," Erik said.

As much as she ached to do something, take some action, Dawn said, "Do you mind staying on the wheel? You're doing a great job."

Erik's face brightened and his shoulders relaxed. "Sure. What's the new heading?"

Dawn got him set up with the new heading. "Kick it up a couple of knots. Let's get this shit over with."

"How long?" Meg asked.

"Twenty minutes, not more. But it doesn't make sense."

"What do you mean?

"As a place to do the exchange. It's out in the open. There's nowhere to run. Nowhere to hide."

Meg pushed a strand of hair off her face. "So we'll know who they are, be able to identify them."

"And their boat," Erik said.

"Right." Dawn paced. "I don't like it. In the movies the only time the bad guys don't care if you see their faces is when they plan to kill you."

The instant the words were out of her mouth, she regretted them.

Meg sucked in a breath and her face paled. "How can we protect ourselves? Maybe it's time to call in the CG?"

"Coast Guard?" Erik asked.

"Yes." Meg went and leaned with her back against the chart table. "What about it, Dawn? This is looking more dangerous by the minute."

"They said they'd kill him." She shoved her hands in her pockets. "I believe them. I say we prepare ourselves and reassess when we get there."

"Prepare ourselves how?" Erik turned and caught her eye. "You have arms on board?"

"I do. I also have the Coast Guard on speed dial."

"It'll be too late to call when we're already there," Meg said. "They need time to reach us. I have Captain Birch's number. Want me to call?"

Dawn extended her arms, palms out. "Let's back up. We're getting ahead of ourselves. All we know for now is they've changed the location. Anyway, being in an open space could work to our advantage."

"How?" Meg crossed her arms.

"I don't know. Let's not panic yet, is all I'm saying." Dawn went into the galley to retrieve the gun she stashed there. Choosing this location for the exchange was too much of a coincidence. Dragging her back to the scene of Joe's death? The voice on the phone hadn't sounded familiar but maybe the ransom was not what they were after. She couldn't shake the feeling she was being toyed with. Possibly drawn into a trap.

Her mind flitted past the ugly thought that Timothy was

involved. It made no sense. If he was involved, if he was setting her up, then why had he led her to the hiding place for his weapon when she was supposed to retrieve money? That seemed like a message. He'd been trying to warn her. Why else would he have her look there?

Dawn tucked the Glock in her waistband and poked her head back into the wheelhouse. "Erik, you carrying?"

He wore a pair of loose khakis and a black T-shirt that wasn't tucked in. Reaching a hand to his lower back, he raised his shirt. She had her answer.

Meg's mouth dropped. "You always walk around armed?"

"Seemed wise," he said, "after our last adventure." He turned back to the sea.

Moving through the wheelhouse, Dawn checked their progress. "Ten minutes." She took the stairs to the forward cabin, grabbed Timothy's gun from where she'd stashed it, and went back to the wheelhouse.

"Never bring a knife to a gunfight," she said, placing the gun on the chart table.

Without a word, Meg scooped it up and weighed it in the palm of her hand. Dawn wondered if she'd protest. During the cruise course, Meg's aim had been off and she'd hit one of the other passengers. She put that down to nerves and rolling waters. It wouldn't be productive to shake Meg's confidence so Dawn kept her mouth shut.

Picking up the binoculars, Dawn scanned the horizon. They were drawing close. Two boats drifted near the dive site. Even from this distance, she easily identified them as charter vessels she'd seen many times before cruising these waters with Joe.

She felt like someone had plunged a knife into her belly. Three months had passed but the grief ripped through her as fresh as the day she'd lost him. Being in these waters was going to rip her heart out. She took a deep breath to calm herself and did what she was good at, what came naturally; she stuffed her feelings.

Meg and Erik deserved for her to be entirely present.

She wasn't going to lose someone else in these waters.

Not today. Not ever.

CHAPTER SEVENTEEN

Timothy licked his lips, the fresher blood tasting as coppery as it smelled. His lips were swollen, split open, caked with dried blood. The inside of his mouth was the Sahara. So dry. He swallowed but it felt like shards of glass raking down his throat. His left eye was swollen closed, a gooey fluid caking his lashes. His cheek burned where the skin was stripped from his cheek by the knife, the resulting blood long-dried against the side of his neck. Bastards.

The zip tie that bound his hands behind his back cut deeply into his wrists and left him no slack to try to get free. He'd seen a YouTube video on how to release himself from zip ties. Wasted time. He'd tried each variation and failed. All the moves he could remember were for hands bound in front and his were bound in back. His captors were assholes but not idiots. Small comfort.

He rolled farther onto his side to relieve the pressure on his lower arm. Every muscle in his body throbbed. He suspected his shoulder was dislocated. Each breath hurt. At least one rib was cracked, or broken, and the pulsing in his nose was unrelenting. Hearing voices, he stilled himself and watched, ready to play dead.

The men strode past him, one of them planting a half-assed kick to his gut on the way by. He gritted his teeth, remained silent.

"What was that for?"

"Why not? He's out cold. Never felt a thing."

Timothy held his breath. He recognized the voice. The men moved into the light. They'd removed their bandanas. Timothy's pulse quickened. It was Miguel and Jose. Miguel, the cruel twisted bastard who had kicked and taunted and humiliated him the last time he'd seen him. Dreams of revenge seared through his veins. He twisted his wrists but succeeded only in digging the zip tie deeper into his tender swollen skin.

"Hey, check this out," Jose said, flicking the screen on his phone. Music blasted out of his cell, the sound tinny in the cavernous space.

Miguel stepped closer, bent his head over the tiny screen. "What is this?"

"I found a back-up copy of the video we did of that model."

"Oh that's great," Miguel said. "Ha, I'm a pretty good dance master, don't ya think?"

"I was thinking more about how good I am with the camera," Jose said, his face tight. "You can't ever give me a compliment?"

"What? You're my wife now? Show me the new one, that's the only one that matters."

Jose huffed but the music stopped and new noise replaced the earlier music. Grunts and muffled cries. If it was porn, it was something twisted.

"Is that the two on the sailboat?"

"Yeah. Good, eh?"

Miguel lowered his head over the little screen. "In the little cove, right?"

"Yeah. Good, right? Good? See how I got the lighting just right? And the angle? Let me fast forward, I want to show you one of the close ups."

Timothy watched the two men gaping at the screen.

Finally, Miguel nodded and clapped Jose on the back. "Good work, Scorsese. But that's enough. Find something better, something more upbeat."

Moments later the strains of boom-chica music and moans familiar to bad porn filled the space. Miguel laughed and grabbed the phone from Jose.

Timothy's head sagged. He struggled to keep his good eye open. If his captors were Miguel and Jose, then kidnapping him was nothing but a ruse, a way to get to Dawn. He didn't like Dawn most days but he sure as hell didn't want to see her walk into this kind of trap.

There was no way to warn her. He was helpless.

The pain overtook him, a fast galloping pony of endless pain, and he drifted down into darkness.

CHAPTER EIGHTEEN

The Papa Joe cut cleanly through the waves, light bouncing off the deck. Meg paced and Dawn continued to scan the horizon with the binoculars. As they closed in on their destination, Erik moved arm's length back from the helm and motioned to Dawn. "You want to take the wheel?"

Dawn nodded and stepped into her spot, grateful for something to focus on.

"See anything that looks off?" Meg asked.

"No. I recognize both of those boats. So far there's nothing out of place here."

"Except whoever we're meeting isn't here," Erik said, pointing out the obvious.

"Yeah, there's that." She pulled the throttle back and coasted with the current. Her phone sat silent on the console beside her.

Someone on the stern of the smaller charter boat waved at them. Dawn grabbed the glasses.

"Anyone?"

"An old friend of Joe's. He offered me a job when Joe died."

"Who's Joe?" Erik asked.

Dawn caught Meg shoot him a look. "The man who used to own this boat," she said.

"It's fine," Dawn said. "In fact, this is where Joe died."

"What?" Meg said. She moved to Dawn's side. "Are you okay?"

The divers from the charters were starting to come up. There was a lot of activity as they were helped aboard the smaller boat. Dawn kept her eyes trained on that. "I'm fine. It's the first time I've been out here since it happened though."

Erik gave her a quizzical look.

"He drowned here," Dawn said simply, by way of explanation.

"Do you think it's coincidence that Timothy's kidnappers sent you here today?" Erik turned to face her, bracing his back against the counter.

"I don't know what to think," Dawn said. Meg's face paled. "But, again, let's not get ahead of ourselves. This is a well-known location. It could easily be a coincidence."

"Then where are they?" Meg pulled her eyes away from Dawn and looked out to sea. "Why aren't they here?"

"I don't have any answers, Meg. We can only wait it out. They'll turn up or they'll call." Dawn's eyes dipped to her phone. They'd been drifting for over ten minutes. The smaller charter boat pulled away, all their divers aboard. A second group of divers started to surface and re-board the second boat.

"Erik probably doesn't know the legends that surround this reef," Meg said.

"What legend?" Dawn asked.

Color tinged Meg's cheeks. "I thought you'd know. Given, well, everything."

"I didn't grow up here," Dawn said. "I'm still piecing things together as far as local history goes. Treasure comes to mind." She remembered most of what Joe had told her, but at the time her mind had been on other things.

Erik's eyes lit up. "Treasure? Do tell."

"Yes, tell us," Dawn said. Anything to keep her mind off the excruciating endless waiting.

"The story is that there's a shipwreck near this reef. Supposedly a Spanish Galleon carrying gold and silver. For years, you couldn't come through here without tripping over treasure hunters. Or that's what my parents told me. They were divers and we spent most weekends on the water.

"They always pointed out this reef as a great dive site, but when I was growing up this whole area was protected."

"But they're diving here now," Erik said.

"We're outside the protected area here. Much closer in and they'd need permits," Dawn explained, remembering the day she first met Captain Cutter, her new guardian angel. He'd come aboard to see Dylan's permit.

"Right," Meg said. "Things have relaxed a little over the years. The reef itself it still protected but you can dive farther out."

"Is the attraction still the shipwreck?" Erik asked.

"Most of the charters play up that angle," Dawn said. "Tourists eat that stuff up."

"Like I said, it's a good dive site," Meg said. "My parents loved coming out here."

Erik leaned up against the chart table, looking disappointed. "That's not much of a legend."

"You look at me now and you probably see the girl next door, right?" Meg looked squarely at Erik. "Never say shit if I had a mouth full of it?"

Erik laughed. "You just did say it."

Reaching out, Meg cuffed him on the upper arm and glanced over at Dawn. Intrigued, Dawn gestured for her to continue.

"When we were teenagers, we used to come out here to dive at night. We were curious, I suppose, and always happy to flirt with danger at that age. My brother was pretty rebellious, he was always getting us into stuff like that.

"We took turns staying on board, while the rest of us dove. Somebody had to keep an eye out for other boats and the Coast Guard. So one night, I'm the one to stay aboard and my brother's best friend tells me a story just before he goes over." Meg paused and drummed her fingers against the wood.

"Come on then," Erik said.

"Wait." Dawn pointed to a boat approaching from the south. She looked through the binoculars but once she'd fixed them in her sights, they swung to the west. While Meg had been talking, the second charter had pulled anchor and was pulling out of the area as well. She slid her phone closer, then tipped her chin at Meg.

Meg picked up her drink and took a sip. "My parents had always told us the area was closed because of the heavy boat and dive traffic, searching for treasure, and the damage it caused to the reef."

"Makes sense," Dawn said.

"This boy told me the real reason was that someone was murdered out here."

CHAPTER NINETEEN

THIS BOY TOLD ME THE REAL REASON WAS THAT SOMEONE WAS murdered out here.

Meg's words echoed through the cabin, eddying like the breeze blowing through the wheelhouse.

Dawn grabbed for a shadow memory edging into her consciousness, fighting for her attention. Something Joe had said.

"The plot thickens," Erik said. "Go on."

"Late one night, two boats showed up at the same time, and one of the crew ended up being shot. The body washed ashore on the beach several days later with a hole in his forehead."

"Gruesome," Erik said.

Dawn's mouth was dry, she reached for her drink. Joe had spoken almost those exact same words. "Then what?"

"He told me the reason the area was protected was because it was haunted by the murdered guy and then he went diving and left me on the boat by myself. I was sixteen. It was terrifying. Every slight whistle of wind had me ready to jump overboard."

Erik laughed. "That's exactly the kind of story I would have told a girl I liked when I was that age. Your brother's friend had a crush on you."

Meg blushed. "As it turned out, yes. We dated for a while."

"Let me guess. He came up earlier than the others to keep you company since you were so scared."

Meg laughed. "Teenage boys are that transparent, are they?"

"Certainly when you've been one, they are." Erik smiled sheepishly.

"But the story about the man being shot, was it true?" Dawn asked.

"It's definitely true that a body was found on the beach with a bullet hole in the head. The rest is mostly rumors. There's been a lot of different stories over the years."

"Such as?" Dawn asked.

Meg took a deep breath. "The main story was that there were three boys, teenagers, maybe seventeen or eighteen, who were responsible for the death."

"Were they ever charged?" Erik asked.

"Nobody was charged. Immediately after the body was found, all three left the area."

"I didn't know that part," Dawn said, slanting a look at Meg.

"Wait. You knew this story?" Meg asked. She crossed her arms and fixed her eyes on Dawn.

"Joe did tell me that there was a lot of boat traffic, and with so many people around, the reef got chewed up. It's one of the main reasons this area was closed."

"But the shooting? Did he tell you about that?" There was a tremor in Meg's voice.

"He said two boats showed up at the same time and one of the crew ended up being shot." Dawn's eyes strayed to the spot on the bow where they'd had lunch that day. The last meal they'd shared. Sandwiches and chips. She wished he was here to advise her now.

"But not more?" Meg pushed.

"No." Dawn shrugged. "We were more concerned about the guys we had on the charter that day. The guys who were diving." She glanced at the time. Twenty minutes had passed. Still no one to meet them and still no call. She was getting antsy. Waiting didn't work for her.

She stared back at Meg, who looked like her face was about to cave in. "Why? What more is there?"

"I just find it ironic that your friend Joe died here is all."

"I don't understand. Ironic, how?"

"They never proved anything, but the rumor was that Joe was one of the three boys out here that night."

CHAPTER TWENTY

Something squeezed hard inside of Dawn. Her throat closed as she gulped in a breath.

"Joe was one of the men out here that night?" Joe's words on his last day came back to her: *Are you going to repeat everything I say?*

Meg looked over her shoulder, then she seemed to force herself to meet Dawn's eye. "It doesn't mean anything. Like I said, just a rumor."

"Rumor." There she went again. Repeating words. On the console beside her, the phone buzzed. She scooped it up and opened the text.

An animated ghost danced across the small screen.

Erik leaned over and glanced at her phone. He cocked a brow. "Still a coincidence?"

Her text pinged a second time. She blocked Erik's view with her shoulder. The movie poster for *The Way We Were* flashed on her screen. There was no room for doubt anymore. Sending her to this location was not a coincidence. Whoever took Timothy knew about Joe dying here.

"What is it?" Meg asked. "You're sheet white. Do you need something? Water?"

Dawn shook her head. Her phone rang and she answered.

"Ms. Devon, enjoying your afternoon?"

"What the hell do you want?" She hissed. "If you want the money for Timothy, let's meet and make our exchange."

"All in good time, Ms. Devon. You don't strike me as the impatient type."

"Clearly you don't know me as well as you think you do."

"I think we both know that isn't true. I realize you have a penchant for self-delusion but I know considerably more about you than you could imagine."

Dawn's fingers gripped the phone tightly. She wanted to throw the offensive thing overboard. Drown out the words. Have this whole day dissolve into the mist. *"Penchant?* We're bringing out the million-dollar words now, are we?"

"Nah, that's just a ten-thousand-dollar word." His laugh blasted through the speaker. She pulled the phone away from her ear.

"Let's complete our business," she said, willing her voice to stay steady. "Where are you?"

"We're on our way, but there's been a slight change in plans."

Dawn filled her lungs with air and let it out slowly.

"Still there, Ms. Devon?"

"Hanging on your every word."

"Good girl."

Her nails dug into the palm of her hand. If she wanted to get Timothy out of this alive, she could not let this asshole get under her skin.

His laugh filtered through the phone again. "Watch for another text from me," he said. "We'll be meeting you elsewhere."

With that the line went dead. Dawn didn't know if she was

scared, confused, insulted or just plain angry. She settled on anger, tinged with fear, and stared down at her phone waiting for the next message.

CHAPTER TWENTY-ONE

Standing at the wheel, Dawn kept her focus squarely on the screen of her phone, refusing to meet either of Meg's or Erik's worried glances. She was vaguely aware of the faint cry of seagulls in the background, the sharp tang of salt in the air. When her phone buzzed, she stared down at the coordinates. A chill ran through her body despite the heat.

What game is this?

Without a word, she pushed the throttle forward and set her heading.

Meg spoke first. "You want me to find something for you on the charts?"

Dawn twitched her head once to the right and fixed her eye on the horizon.

"You know where we're going next?" Erik asked.

She tipped her chin. "I do."

"And you need nothing from us?" Meg said.

"For the moment, no. Why don't you guys get some air?" Out of the corner of her eye, she watched Meg and Erik exchange a look. Erik shrugged and they moved away through the galley toward the stern.

The wheelhouse felt mercifully empty without them. Like she could swing a cat. Two cats. Hell, a chorus line of cats.

Dawn released the tight hold she'd had on her emotions and let the anxiety racing up through her, threatening to burst through her mouth in a primal scream, ride roughshod over her. Her hands gripped the wheel to steady her shaking legs. Her breath came fast and jagged. Her blood pounded in her ears.

She could barely believe how this thing was unfolding. The stuff of nightmares. That voice. It didn't sound like someone she knew, and yet, it was so familiar. How could he know so much about her? She tensed as she remembered his cruel laugh.

Sending her back to the scene of Joe's death had been some kind of message. What exactly, she couldn't be sure. She closed her eyes, breathed deep and struggled to get a grip on her reaction.

And now, they were sending her to the cove where things had gone sideways on her last charter.

Her suspicions were cemented. There was no longer any doubt in her mind that something larger was at stake than a simple kidnapping.

"Dawn." She turned to find Erik stepping through the wheelhouse door. Meg came in behind him. "This area looks familiar. This is where we came last time, right?"

There was no point trying to hide it. Neither of them was stupid. "It is."

"So they're sending us back to the cove where those men held us captive," Meg said, crossing her arms in front of her. She widened her legs but her body language didn't fool Dawn for a second. Meg was nervous. With good reason.

"Correct."

"Why would they do that?" Meg asked.

"Weren't they after you last time?" Erik asked.

Dawn swiveled toward him. "Why would you think that?"

"I heard Timothy say it." He paused and Dawn glared at

him. "You think this is about you again? I mean, maybe they want you, not Timothy. Maybe the kidnapping is a ruse."

Dawn bit her tongue. She'd been wondering the same thing.

Erik pressed. "Maybe Timothy is in on it and what they really want is you. Not the ransom at all."

Meg opened and closed her mouth like a grounded fish.

"Then why bother asking for the ransom?" Dawn said.

"Leverage? I mean, ten thousand dollars? For ransom? Hardly seems worth the effort." Erik shrugged.

"I was thinking the same thing. It's so little money. Really, none of this makes sense." For not the first time today, she was glad she wasn't out here alone.

"It just seems like... sending you to where Joe died, and now, sending you back to this other cove is some sort of a message."

Freaking Erik. Was he reading her mail, or what? She nodded. "I know."

"So what's the message?" Erik said.

"That I don't know."

"No." Meg interrupted them. They both swiveled to look at her.

"No what?" Dawn said.

"I don't think Timothy is involved. It looks like they're actually hurting him. I mean, all those photos with him bleeding and beat up."

"Timothy's desperate for money," Dawn said. "He might go along with it, especially if he had no choice."

"It's only ten grand. They'd have to split it how many ways? He's letting them beat the crap out of him for a couple of grand? Maybe even less? I don't buy it." Agitated, Meg started to pace again, her legs carrying her across the wheelhouse and back again. "Look, I'm not a huge fan of Timothy, certainly not an enemy either, hell, I barely know the man." She stopped, took a breath, and fixed Dawn with a stare. "It seems unlikely is all."

It came back to the money. It wasn't a lot. How could it be the ransom they were after? Why hadn't she seen it sooner? They were after her.

What was she going to do about it? Keep going? Still try to rescue Timothy? At this point, she could be the one that needed rescuing.

"Meg's right," she said. "We keep going."

CHAPTER TWENTY-TWO

Sunlight slanted off the bow. Dawn powered back as she eased the Papa Joe around the point of the cove where they were to meet. The phone had been suspiciously silent. You could cut the air in the wheelhouse with a wet mackerel. Erik shifted his weight constantly between one leg and the other and Meg hadn't stopped her interminable pacing. They were all keyed up. The only thing they had going for them at this point was daylight.

"Spot anything?" Dawn's eyes swept the cove. At the north end, a small sailboat rested at anchor. She put the boat into neutral and coasted. "What do you think?"

"It's the only other craft in here," Meg said.

"Should we go over or wait to hear from them?" Erik glanced over at Dawn, his hands clenching the counter in front of him.

"I'm not sure," Dawn said. She glanced down at her phone. "Let's give it a few minutes."

She turned the wheel back toward the opening to the cove, and idled in a large loop. Energy coursed through her. Fear was the enemy. She was tired of waiting for things to happen. These guys had been pulling her strings since lunch time. She made a decision.

"We're going over." She corrected course and pointed the bow toward the sailboat. It sat peacefully on its anchor, the surface dead calm.

"It doesn't look like there's anyone on board," Erik said, looking through the binoculars.

"Looks can be deceiving," Dawn said.

"The hatch is closed," Erik reported. "The sails are stowed and I don't see a dingy. I'm pretty sure there's no one there."

Dawn continued on her course, turning to glide up alongside the small boat. She grabbed the handset for the PA. "Hello," she called out.

"Looks empty, Dawn. There's nobody there." Meg stepped up beside her. "Now what?"

"I don't know." Dawn chewed on her lower lip, gazing past the sailboat to the shore beyond. "Where would they have gone? Do you see a dingy on the shore anywhere?"

They all scanned the shore, but there was nothing.

Dawn circled. After twenty minutes, she cut the power and they drifted. The sun was sliding toward the horizon with enough haze in the air to promise a spectacular sunset. Dawn couldn't have cared less.

"Maybe we go aboard," Erik said.

Dawn grunted. "No. We can't board someone else's boat. You're right, there's no one there. We wait. It's the only option."

As if on cue, Dawn's phone pinged as a new text came in.

CHAPTER TWENTY-THREE

DAWN GRABBED HER PHONE AND SCANNED THE TEXT: *THIRD time's the charm.* She resisted the urge to throw the damn thing out the window. Instead, as it pinged again, she swore and passed it to Meg. "Can you find this on the chart, please?"

While Meg stepped away, Dawn turned the ignition, looped in another wide circle, and cruised out of the cove. She headed south. At the table, Erik and Meg were having trouble pinpointing their new destination.

"Can I help with anything?"

"It just seems to be another location in the middle of nowhere," Meg explained.

"Erik, take the wheel."

"You bet." He stepped over and Dawn joined Meg, following her finger as Meg pointed out the location. She double-checked the coordinates. "Here's the problem," she said. She turned the chart and showed Meg where they were heading.

"I'm afraid to ask, but is that another location that has personal meaning for you?"

Dawn smiled wryly. "Thankfully not. I've never been there.

Sailed up close to there a few times, but never to the eastern side of the island."

"Do you know what's there?"

"Hopefully Timothy. That'll be enough for me." She leaned against the table and tried to will the tension out of her muscles.

Meg dropped her voice until she could barely be heard over the diesel. "You don't really think Timothy is setting you up, do you?"

"I hope not." She thought back to finding Timothy's gun. If anything, he was sending her a message. A warning.

Meg drummed her fingers on the table. "Feels like we've been going in circles for hours." She sought out Dawn's eye. "I'm going a little stir crazy."

"Me, too," Dawn said. "Hungry?"

"Again?"

She shrugged. "I just thought it would be something to do."

Meg laughed. "I'm good. Unless you want a sandwich or something."

"I don't think I could eat." She swiveled. "Erik? Something to eat?"

He laughed, his lean body turning toward them. "I'm a guy. I can always eat."

"Fine," Meg said. "I'll make some sandwiches."

CHAPTER TWENTY-FOUR

Erik and Meg sat on the bow eating sandwiches and sharing a bag of chips. Except for the setting sun, it was a mirror image of Dawn's last lunch with Joe. She steeled herself and double-checked the time to their new location. The sooner this day was over, the better.

The radio above her head crackled to life. A distress call. She turned up the volume. A pleasure craft with engine trouble. She noted their location. It wasn't far. She waited, hoping someone else would respond.

The sun was slipping below the horizon. She watched for the fabled flash of green. Nothing. The reflection flared watery pink against the water. The call came over the radio again. This time both Meg and Erik heard it, and came inside.

"What is it?" Meg asked. "They calling again?"

"No, it's the radio. A distress call from another boat. I'm hoping someone else will respond and help them."

"Is it something serious?" Meg pushed a strand of hair off her forehead.

"It doesn't sound like it." The three of them stood staring at the radio.

The call came again. Dawn swore softly under her breath and turned the wheel to an east heading.

"How much will this delay us?" Erik said.

"I don't know, except it's not really optional. We can't leave them out here with night falling." She grabbed the mic, responded to the call and let them know they were on their way.

"What if it's a trick? Or a pirate?" Meg said.

"Twisty," Erik said.

Meg jammed her fists against her hips and faced him. "Pretty sure you were on the same cruising course as I was, last time we were both on this boat. I wouldn't say it's completely out of the question."

His brow furrowed. "Maybe not. Dawn, maybe we should let someone else take the call."

"We can get to them in the next fifteen minutes. Let's just get it done." She pushed the throttle forward. It was entirely possible that Meg was right and it was a trap. It could be a set up from Timothy or the kidnappers to steal the ten grand they knew she had on board. She pushed her paranoia down and was happy the current was with them, it would lessen the time out.

———

"There," Meg said. She lowered the binoculars and passed them to Dawn.

Dawn raised the glasses. The small pleasure craft bobbed on the waves. She steered a few degrees to the south and radioed they were in sight and would reach them within ten minutes.

"Erik, you're armed. Stay vigilante in case this is a set up."

He nodded, a quick downward jut of his chin.

Meg started to pace.

"It's probably nothing," Dawn said. "Just hedging our bets, is all." She didn't like being out this time of day. Most pleasure boats headed back to shore after sunset. Night was an unpredictable time in these waters. If there was going to be trouble, it most often showed up under the cloak of darkness.

The small boat was less than half a mile off her bow when her phone pinged. She glanced at the text: *ETA*.

She passed the phone to Meg. "Text back and say we're delayed. ETA TBD."

"TBD?" Meg poked at the keyboard.

"To be determined."

She grimaced. "They're not going to like that. Sure you want to provoke them?"

"I don't give a rat's ass at this point," Dawn said. Meg raised a brow and Dawn forced a half-smile. "Sorry, just send it."

The phone pinged back immediately. Dawn started at Meg's sharp intake of breath and extended her hand.

Another photograph of Timothy. He was lying on his back, barely conscious by the look of it, his face purple and his eyes bulging, a large boot pushing down on his throat.

"Tell that asshole we're answering a distress call and will be there as soon as possible."

Meg took back the phone and typed in the message.

The phone pinged a response. "He says he wants an ETA within twenty minutes." Meg said. Dawn took her phone and slid it in her back pocket.

"You ready Erik?"

Erik had been checking his gun. He shoved it into the waistband at the small of his back. "You bet." Dawn wondered where the mild-manner guy she'd dubbed the Professor had gone. At the same time, she was grateful for this side of Erik.

"How about you both get ready to take a line. We'll cruise up alongside and see what we're dealing with. Erik, you take the bow. Meg, you know where the bumpers are. Put a couple down along the port side, near the stern."

As they left the cabin, Dawn throttled back and picked up

the binoculars. A man in his mid-twenties waved frantically, holding a ball cap to get their attention. She reached overhead and switched the PA on. "We'll come up along your starboard," she said. "Get ready with a line."

She idled against the current until the small craft drifted in along her port side. On the bow, Erik kept one hand behind his back. Dawn made a quick assessment. The man's young wife sat on a bench seat cradling an infant. The cubby in the bow didn't look big enough to secret anyone else out of sight.

The man threw a line up to Erik who walked it back toward the stern to tie them off.

Dawn shut down and stepped out through the port door.

The young man peered up at her. "Josh Jones," he said. "Thanks for coming."

"Anyone else on board?" Dawn looked toward the cubby in the bow.

"Just the three of us," he said.

"You mind if we confirm that?" Dawn said.

Josh and his wife exchanged a look. "It's just us. We broke down and need help."

His wife interrupted. "Come look if you want."

"Jump down and check it out, Erik." Erik nodded and Josh gripped the gunwales of the Papa Joe to hold his boat steady while Erik stepped down.

Erik poked his head into the cubby and addressed Dawn. "Empty. Like he said."

"What seems to be the problem, Josh?" Dawn leaned against the door.

"We were cruising along, everything was fine, and the engine sputtered and quit."

"This ever happen before?" Erik was already leaning over the engine at the back.

In the fading light, it was hard to make out Josh's features but Dawn saw his face redden. "It's my father-in-law's boat. He lent it to us for the day."

"And my father is going to kill us if we don't get it back in one piece," the woman said. The baby started to stir, and she rocked it in her arms.

"We'll try to get you on your way again," Dawn said.

"I'm Melissa," the woman said. She was younger than Dawn by about eight or nine years. "I've always heard it's a bad idea to be out here at night. I'm a little bit scared."

"We'll figure out what the problem is."

"If you don't, can we come with you?" Melissa clasped the baby tighter to her chest. "Maybe you could tow us somewhere?"

CHAPTER TWENTY-FIVE

MEG, WHO HAD BEEN LEANING AGAINST THE GALLEY CABIN, coughed. "Erik will figure it out," she said.

In Dawn's back pocket, her phone vibrated and pinged. She stepped into the wheelhouse and opened the text: *ETA!*

Unknown. We're helping someone with engine troubles.

Ditch them. Get over here.

Should I call the Coast Guard to help them?

Dawn waited for his response. Fifteen seconds passed, then thirty. Just when she was ready to text again to say she had no intention of involving the CG, his response came.

Finish up and get on your way.

Dawn jammed the phone back in her pocket and stepped over to the charts. If it had been a couple of guys, or even just the couple, she might have left them, but it was going to be difficult to leave a small baby in the middle of the ocean with night falling. The woman had offered a viable solution. It would be simple enough to bring them aboard and tow them somewhere. Simple and the decent thing to do.

The other alternative, of course, was to call the Coast Guard. But they'd have to wait for them to arrive. She had no idea what their response time would be. And she was sure Timothy's captors were monitoring the radio. If she made a call to the CG, they'd know about it. Meg probably had Birch's number—they could use her cell to call him. But then what? Could she risk having to explain any of it?

No, she'd have to deal with what was in front of her in the most efficient way she could manage. Meantime, Timothy's life hung in the balance.

She scanned the charts looking for somewhere nearby to tow them. Tracing her finger over the chart, she searched for somewhere enroute to her destination where she could drop them. The problem was, most of these little islands were either uninhabited or privately owned.

On the other boat, the outboard sputtered. She stepped back outside.

"How much longer, Erik?"

"I'm not sure what the problem is. Give me another few minutes."

"Hon," Melissa said, rocking the baby in her arms, "the Captain said she'd tow us in if we can't get underway again."

Dawn cleared her throat. "I didn't say that actually. We're not able to stay much longer. Did you call the Coast Guard?"

"I sent the distress call," Josh said. "On the radio. The one that you answered."

"Yes, but there's also a phone number for the Coast Guard. Do you have a working cell?"

Melissa stood up. "You're not planning to leave us out here? If the Coast Guard was nearby, wouldn't they have answered our distress call?"

"Not necessarily. If they knew we were responding, then maybe they're dealing with more urgent matters."

"Urgent matters?" Melissa's voice rose. "I'd call me being stranded with my baby overnight on a boat that doesn't work an urgent matter. We're in the middle of nowhere and—"

"Calm down, babe," Josh said, squeezing her wrist and guiding her over to the side. "Sit. Let the man work on the engine." He cast a glance of reproach toward Dawn.

Erik popped his head up. "Hey Josh, try it again."

Josh stepped to the console and turned the key in the ignition. The engine sputtered and quit.

"Sounds to me like it's not getting fuel," Erik said, peering up at Dawn. Beside her, Meg had started to rock from foot to foot. They were all aware of the time ticking away. "Want to come down and take a look?"

Dawn hopped down and moved to the console. "Are you carrying spare gas?"

"There's a can here," Josh said, reaching below the stern. "Feels empty." He rocked the can, a small amount of liquid sloshed against the sides.

"Meg, can you check under the stern of our boat and bring me a small gas can?"

Twilight was fading, a strip of purple against the horizon the last of the light. If this didn't work, she'd have to tow them somewhere.

Moments later, Meg returned and passed the can down to Josh. Dawn had him place it near the one that was connected and changed the lines. She stepped to the console and turned the ignition. The engine started, ran several seconds, then coughed and died. "Pump it," she said to Erik.

Erik reached around, pumped the gas line. Dawn turned the ignition. This time, the engine caught, sputtered, then stayed running. Not a purr exactly, but a relatively steady idle.

"Probably dirty gas," Dawn said.

Josh clasped her hand. "Thank you. Thank you for coming out here."

"No worries." She caught Erik's eye and tilted her head toward the boat. "I want you to head straight to shore. Never mind trying to get home, head to the nearest harbor on the mainland. Got it?"

"Yes," Josh said.

"Thank you," Melissa said. She was visibly relieved, her baby asleep in her arms. "I'm sorry about—"

Dawn flicked her wrist and took Meg's hand to climb back onto her own boat. "It's fine. You'll get home safe now."

Josh grabbed the empty gas can and passed it up to Dawn. "Take this. To replace the can you gave us."

Before she could reach for it, Erik grabbed it from Josh and headed to the stern to stow it. Meg untied their line and tossed it down to Josh.

"Put your running lights on," Dawn said. "First harbor. Hear me?"

Josh nodded, turned on the lights and idled away from them. As he pulled away, she stepped into the wheelhouse and fired up the diesel.

"Good grief," Meg said, coming up from the galley. "I couldn't believe it when she said they would come aboard. What a disaster that would have been."

"All good now," Dawn said, turning the boat to their previous heading.

Except it wasn't all good. Helping them had been a delay they could ill afford. They still had to find Timothy. The bastard who kept phoning could be leading them on yet another wild goose chase and they'd run out of daylight.

Nightfall was only going to make everything more difficult.

CHAPTER TWENTY-SIX

NIGHT FELL QUICKLY. THE LAST SLIVER OF COLOR ALONG THE horizon replaced by an inky blackness that opened the sky above to fathomless heights. It was a moonless night. More stars than Dawn had ever seen blossomed above as she held steady to her heading and the diesel vibrated the deck beneath her feet. There were moments like this in her life that she'd never forget. Moments so rich in sensory memory that, even as they were unfolding, she knew she would take them to her grave. She only hoped it wouldn't be an early grave.

She guided the Papa Joe along the northern shore of the island, roughly twenty minutes from their destination. In a perfect world, she'd know what lay on the other side. But who the hell needed perfect? Perfect was boring and she'd walked away from any chance of perfect years ago.

The phone had been silent since she'd finally sent the kidnapper her ETA. They were on track to be on time.

At her insistence, Meg and Erik had retreated to the galley. Their chatter had been distracting. To her delight, she discovered she loved being in the darkened wheelhouse, the lights of the console reflecting softly in the window. It was her first time behind the wheel at night with sole responsibility for her boat. Ironically, her first time out without Timothy as her first mate. Necessity was a wonderful teacher. It was gratifying to realize how much more confident she was now that her skills were improving.

The northeast point of the island loomed off the starboard. She left plenty of room and headed south. About a mile down, she passed a sprinkling of lights on the shore. Too small to be a village - in any case there was nothing on the charts - too large to be a private home. Possibly a resort. Beyond that, only miles of dark shoreline and the canopy of stars overhead.

"Hey, guys," she yelled. "Come on up."

Meg came up to the wheelhouse. "We getting close?"

"Five, ten minutes out. Where's Erik?"

"I thought he was right behind me. Probably doing the guy thing off the stern."

"The guy thing?"

Meg shrugged. "Taking a leak, I mean."

Dawn laughed. Not a bad idea. Now she needed the head, too. "Take the wheel a minute?" Meg stepped into her place and Dawn went forward. When she stepped back into the wheelhouse, Erik was there.

She resumed her place behind the wheel. "We're almost there. Any last questions?"

Meg and Erik shook their heads.

"Any last reservations?"

"No," Meg said. "Let's go get him."

Erik tipped his chin. "Agreed."

Dawn picked up her phone and texted: *ETA 5 minutes.*

CHAPTER TWENTY-SEVEN

Two quick bursts of white flashed on the shore, lighting up the night.

"We're here." Dawn brought the power back and idled.

"Now what?" Meg said.

"I'm sure we'll know soon enough." Reaching overhead, she turned on the large spotlight and beamed it on the shoreline. A pebble beach. A small boat. A single figure silhouetted against it.

"Want me to drop anchor?" Erik stepped toward the door.

"Not yet. Let's wait 'til they call." The seconds stretched into minutes. Her palms dampened and she pushed her hand through her hair. "He knows we're here, what is he waiting for?"

"Maybe it's another false location." In the glow of the console lights, Meg's face glinted red and yellow.

"He has to be getting tired of that game by now." Erik leaned against the port door, peering toward shore.

Dawn picked up her phone. Put it down. Picked it up again.

From across the water, they heard a splash. Dawn flicked on the spotlight. The man on the shore pushed the boat into the surf, climbed in, set up his oars and rowed in their direction, each dip of the oar into the calm surface audible.

He took his time, even, steady strokes, occasionally glancing over his shoulder to confirm he was on course. An unnecessary movement since Dawn left the spotlight on, a superhighway of light guiding him to them.

"This is crazy," Meg said. "It's so quiet."

"Almost time to go below." Dawn looked at Erik and Meg. "He thinks I'm alone. Let's keep what little advantage we have."

"We'll be right here," Meg said, backing down the stairs.

"I'll stay up," Erik said. "It's dark. He won't know I'm here. You need some backup."

Dawn shook her head. "Safer this way. Go ahead, it's only one guy. I can handle him."

"We'll be right here," he said, echoing Meg's words as he disappeared below and left her on her own.

She leaned into the port doorway and watched the oars dip rhythmically into the water, the small boat pulling closer with each stroke. She swallowed, her throat dry, and reached for her drink. Another two minutes and the boat would reach her.

"Can you turn off the spotlight?" The voice that carried across the water was soft, slightly accented, with a slight tremor. "Turn your inside cabin lights on."

Dawn stepped inside and complied. She shielded her eyes from the cabin light, not wanting to lose her night vision, and moved back to the door.

The man in the boat bumped up against the hull. "Evening," he said. He looked eighty years old, his face wrinkled and beaten by the sun. His shoulders curved forward, a permanent thing, nothing to do with the oars. He pushed a cap back off his head.

"Where is Timothy?"

"I don't know anything about that," he said. "I was asked to come and pick something up. Hang on. I'm supposed to make a phone call when I arrive."

She stood watching him, her shadow stretching across his boat. He pulled a phone from his pocket, fiddled with it, then said, "I'm here." After a pause, he disconnected and shoved the phone back in his pocket.

Dawn's phone rang. She pulled it from her pocket and answered, keeping her eye on the man in the boat.

"My friend made it, I see." The now familiar voice came through the clear line.

"Do you? Why can't I see you?"

"Figure of speech, Ms. Devon. You shouldn't assume I'm nearby. In fact, it would be unwise to assume anything."

Dawn's heart sank. Of course it would. "Where's Timothy?"

"Hang on." He yelled something in the background, waited for a response. "He's sleeping apparently. On a fine feather bed, no doubt."

"I've had about enough of your games," Dawn said, turning her face away from the man below who was watching her. "Let's make our exchange."

"It's not going to work exactly like that," he said. "My friend there is going to pick up the ten grand. Later, once I have the money, he'll lead you to your friend."

"No. I'm not paying you anything until you deliver him to me."

"Ms. Devon, do I need to remind you that you're not in any position to call the shots?"

"Where is he?"

"Like I said, he's nearby."

"Where are you?"

The man laughed. "You ask a lot of questions. Tell me something, Ms. Devon, how many people have to die before we get your attention?"

"You're not going to kill Timothy." Her jaw tightened. "You must think I'm stupid. Timothy is not the one you want."

"Do tell."

"You didn't go to all this trouble for ten grand."

"It was highly entertaining watching you run around all day. Well worth the trouble, I think."

"Bullshit."

"I'm listening," he said.

"Here's the deal. I'm not coming. I'll give your pal the money and you can let Timothy go. But I'm not coming."

She took a breath. The pause on the line lengthened.

Finally, he spoke, his voice quiet. "Tell me about the cove."

"What? Which cove?"

"The second stop on your journey today."

"You mean where you sent us to waste more of my time?"

"Did I? Tell me about it."

What was it that he wanted? "I've been there before," she said.

"Yes. What else?"

"Nothing else. We waited. You weren't there. There was nothing there."

"Nothing?"

"A sailboat. There was nobody on it."

"Are you sure about that?"

"The sailboat was closed up, there was nobody there." The little guy with the pickaxe started chipping away at Dawn's stomach. Something wicked this way was coming, the turmoil in her gut was rarely wrong.

In the rowboat, the man's phone rang. He pulled it from his pocket. "Yes," he said. He flicked the screen until he found what he was looking for then passed it up to Dawn. "He wanted me to show you this."

The video was already playing. Dawn stared at the screen. At first, it was mostly dark, the camera bouncing around. A small space. Muffled cries and sobbing. She prepared herself for another horrible image of Timothy.

A bright light came on and spotlighted an older couple, shoulder to shoulder, on a narrow bunk. They were both gagged with dirty kerchiefs. The woman was crying, her cheeks wet and glossy. There was a large gash on the man's forehead, his eyes wild, his face beet red. He looked ready to have a heart attack any second.

What fresh hell was this?

The camera panned down, past their shoulders.

Tightly bound to the man's chest was a large bundle of explosives.

CHAPTER TWENTY-EIGHT

WHAT FRESH HELL WAS THIS?

The light in the video was turned off. The screen faded to dark as the video continued to play several seconds more with only the sound of the woman's pitiful muffled cries, like a kitten mewing in a bag. Then the mechanical sound of a ticking clock. Tick, tick, tick. A burst of red filled the screen, like paint being thrown on the camera lens, and the video ended. Subtle. Acid crawled up Dawn's throat. She wanted to throw up.

Dawn's hand shook as she passed the video down to the man in the boat. "Do you know these people?"

His lower lip trembled. Only now did she see the tension and stress in his face. "My brother and his wife," he said. "They own a little sailboat. Please. I don't know what the hell this is about but please, just give me the package I was sent to pick up so he won't kill them."

"What's the name of their boat?"

"Serenity Jane. Named after our mother."

The sailboat in the cove. They'd checked on it while they were there. How could she have known?

Her mind raced. How could she give him the money?

Without it, she'd have no leverage to secure Timothy's safety and get him back.

"Please," the man said. "We're running out of time."

"He's holding a friend of mine, too," she said. "If I give you the package, if I help to save your brother, you have to help me, too."

The man shook his head slowly. "He told me I couldn't agree to anything. Only to bring the package and my relatives would live."

"Look," she said. "It's not negotiable. We can help each other. He's not here. He can't know what we talk about here."

"You don't know him."

Her heart skipped a beat. "You do? Do you know this man?"

"Not personally, no. Only by phone."

"Where are you supposed to take the package?"

He shook his head, the color draining from his face, his eyes darting wildly in all directions. "I can't tell you that. They'll know it was me. None of this will matter if I tell you."

"They won't know it's you. If you want me to give you the package, you're going to have to help me. There's a life in the wind on my side, too. I promise it won't come back to you. Tell me."

The closing tick, tick, tick of the bomb from the last seconds of the video replayed in her head. Her body tense, she waited and watched his face. He met her eye. She didn't back down. Seconds later, his shoulders drooped and he sighed. "Fine, I'll tell you. But get the package first."

Dawn hurried into the galley and grabbed the envelope of cash from the small backpack she'd stashed under the seat. For the first time today, she felt like she was making progress. She'd give up the money but she'd have the element of surprise by showing up when they didn't expect her.

She returned with the money. The man stretched his hand up.

"Location first," she said.

"Package first," he said.

"Look we could do this all day," she said. "Here's the package. Just tell me where you're meeting them. I also know where your brother's sailboat is."

His brow furrowed. "You know where they are?" Before she could respond, his phone rang.

"Leave it," she said.

He ignored her and reached into his pocket. But when his hand was visible again, Dawn found herself staring down the barrel of his pistol.

"Give me the package."

"Don't do this," she said. "We can help each other."

"You don't believe I'll shoot? I'm not losing my family over something like this. Hand down the package."

"I don't think so." Erik's voice came from the bow. He walked along the side toward Dawn, his weapon aimed squarely at the man's head. "Don't do anything stupid. Put your gun down."

"You were supposed to be alone," the man sputtered.

"Put down your weapon." Erik enunciated each syllable in a staccato burst of words.

"You're outnumbered," Meg said. She appeared from the stern and closed in on the other side.

The man's eyes narrowed. He lowered his arm. Dawn outstretched her hand. "Give it here." Reluctantly, he passed her the gun.

"Great timing, guys," she said, exhaling. She hadn't realized she'd been holding her breath.

"What do you think, Dawn? Bring this guy onboard or what?" Erik jumped down into the small rowboat and motioned to the man to sit down. Erik towered over him, gun pointed at the man's face, the other hand gripping the side of the Papa Joe.

"They'll get suspicious if he doesn't go back," Dawn said. "Plus, there are two other lives at stake now, too."

"He doesn't seem disposed to listen to reason," Meg said.

Erik placed his gun against the man's temple. "Perhaps he'll listen now."

"Back down, Erik. This guy is not the enemy," Dawn said.

"He pulled a gun on you," Erik said. "Either we control him or he controls us. Dawn offered you a fair deal. Maybe you've had a chance to reconsider."

The man lowered his chin to his chest. Erik pushed his forehead back with the barrel of the gun. They stared at each other, Erik's eyes blazing, the older man's dancing with fear.

In Dawn's head, the clock was ticking. The longer he stayed out here, the more suspicion it was bound to cause. She hated to be cruel, the man was clearly terrified, but his reluctance to cooperate forced her into a corner.

"Will you help us?" she asked the man.

"I can't," he said.

She sighed. "Tie him up, Erik. Better gag him, too, and then come aboard. We need a new strategy."

CHAPTER TWENTY-NINE

"How long do you think it will be until they start calling again? We can't sit here all night, we need to decide and we need to do it quickly." Erik leaned against the counter in the galley, his leg bouncing, his foot drumming a rhythmic beat against the deck.

"Can you stop that?" Dawn said, the pounding was tapping on her nerves. "If we force him to tell us where the drop is, we have no way of knowing if he's telling the truth."

"Except he wants to save his relatives. Are you sure it's the same sailboat we saw in the cove?" Meg said. She sat hunched on the galley steps, almost doubled over on herself, her elbows resting on her knees.

"Yes. I remember the name. Serenity Jane."

Meg dropped her head in her hands. "Why didn't we look when we were there? We could have saved them."

"Based on what?" Dawn said. "The boat was closed up. How could we know there was a couple with a bomb onboard? And what could we do about a bomb? Do either of you know anything about bombs? I sure don't."

Nervous energy coursing through her body forced Dawn to

her feet. She paced the small space feeling like a caged animal. "Let's see things from his point of view." She ticked off her points on her fingers. "Wanting to save them is all the more reason not to be truthful with us. It's in his best interest to keep his mouth shut. Get the package, get to the drop, and save his brother and sister-in-law." Her eyes bounced around the small cabin, seeking inspiration.

"If we hold him much longer, they're going to know something is up. Then we put both the couple and Timothy at risk," Meg said.

"But why not just hold him?" Erik said. "Force them to come to come to us if they want the ransom."

"No. They'll almost certainly blow up that couple. I don't want that on my conscience. Do you?"

Meg and Erik shook their heads.

"What a mess," Meg said.

"Why don't I go with him?" Both women fixed on Erik.

Dawn shook her head. "Too risky."

Erik put up his palm. "Hear me out. He's in a rowboat. Doesn't it make sense that he's going somewhere nearby?"

"Or he has another boat somewhere," Meg said.

"We didn't see one. We've come down the whole shore."

"I'm with Meg," Dawn said. "He could have another boat farther down this shore. Just because we haven't seen it, doesn't mean it doesn't exist. I mean, how did the rowboat get here? Someone probably dropped him off here. For all we know, they're drifting off shore, just out of our sight, waiting. Honestly, they could be anywhere."

"Maybe," Erik said. "I say I go with him to the drop point. That way he can't screw with us. It's the only thing that covers most of the bases."

"I think Erik's right," Meg said.

"And then what?" Dawn drummed her fingers against the table. Erik started to speak but she held up her hand. A plan was forming but it was like trying to catch smoke. She slapped her palm on the Formica surface then pointed to Erik. "Okay. You go to shore with this guy. Meg will row you in. She'll bring the boat back here and you'll keep us updated."

"Why bring the boat back here?" Meg asked. "What if Erik needs it to get back?"

"Because if they're going somewhere nearby, we need a quiet way to follow," Dawn said. "The rowboat will be perfect for that."

"That's too dangerous for Meg," Erik said. "What if they're waiting on shore?"

"If they're waiting, you're going to need backup," Dawn said. "I'll row you in. Meg can stay out here."

Meg stepped forward. "I'll go. It will only take a few minutes. You cover us from here."

Erik pushed himself off the counter and extended his hand to Dawn. "Give me your phone. I'll sync them to be sure we can stay in touch."

CHAPTER THIRTY

IN THE STILLNESS OF THE NIGHT, THE SONG OF WARBLERS chirping in the trees along the shore floated over the water. Outside the cabin, darkness folded in on them. The blackness was complete, even the shoreline was indistinct. It was like being in a cave or a Hallowe'en haunted house. Dawn felt like something could jump out at them from the shadows at any moment.

Standing to the side with Meg, they waited while Erik climbed down into the rowboat. "You wanna tell him or should I?"

Dawn snorted. "I will." She addressed the man. "What's your name?"

He raised his brows and glared at her.

"Erik, take the gag off."

Erik removed the gag and the man spat over the side. "What the hell," he said.

"Name," Dawn said.

"Bill."

"Okay, Bill. One last time. Tell us where the drop point is."

Dawn folded her arms across her chest. Bill's eyes flicked from her to Erik then back to her.

"I can't do that," he said.

"We're going to find out with or without your cooperation," she said. "Erik will go with you to make the drop."

Bill's eyes flared wide. "No. That's going to get us all killed."

Dawn shrugged. "I don't see another solution. Erik goes with you. They won't know he's there. You make the drop, they take the bomb off your brother, and we'll get our friend. Easy peasy."

Sputtering, Bill couldn't seem to form coherent words.

Erik shoved Bill's shoulder. "Sit in the stern where I can see you."

Bill got up and staggered to the back, unsteady on his feet with his hands tied.

Dawn turned to Meg. "Go ahead," she said.

Erik reached up to help Meg down. "I'll row," he said. "You sit behind me in the bow and make sure you have a clear shot at Bill. And no mistakes like you made with Jenny."

Meg grumbled something under her breath that only Erik heard. Erik barked out a laugh.

"Remember, he's not the enemy," Dawn said. "There's no reason to treat him roughly." She looked Bill in the eye. "As long as he doesn't cause problems."

"He's the enemy if he's making us jump through these hoops," Erik said. He arranged the oars in the oarlocks. Dawn tossed the painter down to Meg.

"Bill, you'll remain safe as long as you cooperate with Erik. Just take him to the drop point. You have my word."

"Their blood will be on your hands," Bill said, scowling up at her.

Exasperated, Dawn rolled her eyes. "And my friend's blood will be on yours."

CHAPTER THIRTY-ONE

DAWN WATCHED ERIK ROW AWAY INTO THE NIGHT WITH Meg and Bill. The rhythmic dipping of the oars sounded peaceful. An illusion. Her head with filled with the interminable ticking from the video and the sensation that the world was about to blow up around her. She understood Bill's fear, but they'd been willing to help him. They could have helped each other.

In her pocket, her phone vibrated. It had been too silent for too long. She cursed and stepped inside.

"What?"

"Ms. Devon, what seems to be the hold up?"

She paced across the wheelhouse. "He's on his way. I'm sure he'll be there shortly."

"And the money?"

"Yes," she hissed. "He has the damn money. Now I want to know that Timothy is all right."

"You want." His voice trembled with laughter. "You're not in a position to be making demands."

Why did he find this so damn amusing? "Look, where and

when are you going to release Timothy to me? I've done every-thing you've asked."

"Not quite everything," he said, his voice like silk.

She had no idea what he meant. "I need to know Timothy's all right. Put him on the phone."

"He's... indisposed. I could send you another photograph."

"No. I want to talk to him."

"Hang on." He yelled to someone in the background. "What's our guest doing right now?"

Dawn held her breath, willing the blood to stop pounding in her ears. Then she heard it. Very faintly in the background, a man's voice she recognized said, "Miguel, boss wants you."

Miguel. The cruel thug who had taken them all hostage the day she'd met Meg and Erik. Dawn's body tensed. There were few people in the world she detested more than Miguel.

And the voice was none other than Jose's, his less than bright sidekick. She should have known they would be involved somehow. This cinched it. The whole thing—the money, the kidnapping—was all a set up. It was a trap and she was walking right into it.

But it made no sense. If they wanted her, why take the money and run?

On the other end of the line, a hushed conversation was taking place, the words and voices indistinct.

"I'm afraid Timothy is not able to come to the phone at the moment. He's watching *The Bachelorette*." The man snorted.

"Tell me when and where you will drop Timothy," she said, her voice flat.

"I haven't been paid yet," he said.

"The money will get to you soon."

"And when it does, we'll talk again."

With that, the line went dead.

Dawn tossed the phone onto the bench and sat down beside it.

Miguel. Jose.

Fear gripped her. Meg and Erik were out there in the night and those monsters were somewhere nearby.

CHAPTER THIRTY-TWO

DAWN STOOD ON THE BOW, PEERING THROUGH THE DARK toward shore. The clank of the oars against the gunwales drawing closer. She stepped into the wheelhouse and flashed the spotlight on for two seconds to guide Meg back, then killed the light and went back outside.

The boat continued to approach, the splash of the oars dipping into the water the only noise against the rich backdrop of cicadas and warblers.

"Where are you?" Meg's stage whisper reached her across the water.

"Here," Dawn called back.

Moments later, Meg almost plowed into the side of the Papa Joe. "Whoa, you're here," Dawn said, kicking her foot down to hold the boat off. "Pass me a line."

Meg stowed the oars and passed the painter up to Dawn, then grabbed for the gunwale. Dawn reached out and helped her back onboard, relieved she'd made it back safely. "How did it go?"

"I dropped them and came right back. There was nobody around."

Dawn heaved a sigh of relief. It had been stupid to send Meg in there.

"Get your gear," Dawn said. "Change of plans."

"Where we headed? What do I need?"

"Just the gun. We're going to follow them on foot."

"I thought we were going to wait for Erik to call us and follow them with the rowboat."

"Hell, no," Dawn said. She couldn't bear to wait longer. It was time to take action.

"Don't you trust Erik?"

"There's too much at stake. They just walked away with ten grand and there's no guarantee we'll see Timothy again."

"Or Erik," Meg said, her mouth downturned.

"Right. We're going after them, he might need back up." She patted her pockets for the tenth time to be sure she had everything she needed. "If we find Timothy quickly, we might be able to get back to the sailboat before that bomb goes off. I'm tired of waiting around. Grab your stuff."

"I'm already armed," Meg said. "Anything I can help you with?"

"Nope. I'm ready," Dawn said. "I'll just lock up."

"Will anyone bother things out here?" Meg asked doubtfully.

"Probably not. Better safe than sorry though." Dawn stepped inside and pulled air into her lungs. She was anxious and couldn't squash down the fire in her belly. Leaving the Papa Joe unattended in these waters was a big risk. Anything could happen. It seemed secluded and quiet but that could change in an instant if someone came along.

It also meant leaving behind the money. Once again, she thought of the forty thousand dollars in cash she'd stowed below. It would be crazy for her to take it along. Still, it felt insane to leave it behind. Both options were fraught with risk.

Leaving it behind seemed the lesser of the two given she'd need her full concentration and focus for what lay ahead of them.

She'd already locked most of the doors. She made one more quick sweep, then closed and locked the back galley door. Without hesitating longer, she jumped down into the small boat and Meg rowed them toward shore.

"Did you see where they went?" she asked.

"Apparently, there's an abandoned resort on the southern end of the island. They entered the woods at the south end of the beach."

"An abandoned resort? Did Bill say anything else? About who he was meeting?"

Meg shook her head once, a curt no.

"Anything?"

"He barely spoke. Erik either." Meg pulled steadily on the oars with a strong stroke. The little boat glided over the water.

"You're good at that," Dawn said.

Meg shrugged. "Like I said, a lot of time on the water with my parents when I was a kid."

"If you're tired, I'll take over."

"I'm fine," she said. "Or is that your not so subtle way of asking me to pick up the pace?"

"Yeah, that. Faster is better than quiet right now."

Meg nodded and put her back into it, pulling them faster toward shore. Minutes later, they beached the small boat and ran down the pebbled beach to the southern end. Dawn flicked on her flashlight and passed one to Meg. A minute later, Meg hissed her name. She'd found the path. Dawn took the lead and they jogged down the path, careful to avoid twigs or anything that might make noise and alert Erik or Bill they were being followed.

The path was overgrown. Gigantic leaves dripping with moisture slapped into her face. At times she ducked and bent low to make her way through. Bits of leaves and stems littered the ground. Someone had been through recently with a machete.

Ten minutes down the path, Dawn stopped to catch her breath. Meg skidded to a stop behind her. "Still nothing?"

"They had a head start," Dawn said. "But we should be getting close. You good to keep going?"

Meg nodded. "My extra training for the CG is coming in handy already."

"Yeah, it is," Dawn said. Her extra time in the gym was also paying off. "Let's be careful going forward so they don't hear us."

She turned and moved down the path more slowly, paying special attention to things underfoot. She had no idea how close they were to their destination and they couldn't afford to be heard.

As she ran, her mind raced along with her, presenting her with so many different scenarios for when they arrived, that she couldn't keep up. Timothy would already be dead. Bill would somehow overtake Erik and he'd also need to be rescued. The kidnappers would take the money and never tell her where to find Timothy. Or send her on another wild goose chase to find him.

After several minutes, she paused again. She could hear Meg coming behind her. To avoid whiplash from the overgrown plants, Meg had stayed back a good distance.

Dawn stood, the jungle pressing in around her, trying to separate the sound of Meg approaching and any sound farther to the south. Any sign of nearby life. The stillness was broken by a small cry followed by a thud. Frozen in place, ears peeled, she waited. Meg no longer approached. Something had happened. Torn, she looked at the path before her and the path behind her.

In her head came the tick, tick, tick of the bomb on Bill's brother's chest. The flare of red from the video flashed before her eyes. The pull to continue on was strong.

She pivoted and headed straight back the way she'd come, back to check on Meg.

CHAPTER THIRTY-THREE

TEN YARDS. TWENTY YARDS. TWENTY-FIVE YARDS BACK ON the path, Dawn came upon Meg. She was sprawled face down, her neck twisted at an odd angle, her arms reaching forward, one leg tucked under her and the other with a vine wrapped around her ankle.

"Meg!" Dawn knelt beside her, her fingers gingerly probing her neck to check for a pulse. Her pulse was fine, her breathing regular. She was afraid to move her. She checked down along her body for breaks. Despite the crooked and awkward angles, there seemed to be no broken bones. Digging in her pocket, she extracted her multi-tool and sliced through the vines wrapped around Meg's ankle.

Once she'd freed Meg's leg, she crawled back to her head. She needed her awake. "Meg." She leaned over, her mouth close to Meg's ear. Nothing. She tried again. "Meg." She patted her cheek. Softly at first, then a solid slap. Meg's eyelids fluttered.

"Wake up. Come on, I need you awake."

"What?" Meg opened her eyes, her gaze unfocused. "Where am I?"

Dawn leaned over into Meg's line of vision. "It's me. Dawn. I'm here."

"Where is here?"

"We're in the jungle on the island. Remember? We were on the boat."

"We were on the boat?"

"Meg, snap out of it." Reaching behind her shoulder, she half pulled, half lifted her to a sitting position. She was worried she might have hit the ground hard enough to have a concussion.

Meg coughed, reached up to her neck and groaned. "Oh man, I couldn't stop myself. It was like I was flying through the air."

"Do you think you can get up?"

"You go on without me," Meg said. "Go, you're losing time."

Dawn slanted a look toward the path. Meg was right. Each minute that ticked by she was farther away from Erik and Bill and any chance she had of finding Timothy. "Not until I know you're all right. Can you stand?"

"I'm not sure. My ankle's on fire."

"I checked you. I don't think you broke anything."

"That's small consolation at the moment," Meg said, a tear streaming down her cheek. "Frankly, it feels like everything in my body is broken."

"Come on," Dawn said, sliding an arm beneath Meg's. "Mostly I think you had the air knocked out of you. Let's get you on your feet." Bracing herself, she pushed until she had Meg standing up.

"I can't." Meg lifted her right ankle. "Are you sure it's not broken?"

Dawn scanned the trees beside the path. "There," she said, pointing to a large palm three yards away. "Let's get you over there so you have something to lean up against." She shuffled forward, supporting Meg's weight. Meg hopped along beside her, grunting with exertion. As Dawn brought her alongside the palm, Meg leaned forward and vomited, retching until there was nothing left.

"Go," she croaked. "This is taking too long."

"Will you be okay?"

"I will be." She put some weight on her ankle. "It's hellish sore, but probably only sprained. I want you to go. I'll catch up."

Dawn raised her brow. That seemed unlikely.

"I will," Meg said. "And if not, you know where to find me."

Dawn's eyes strayed to the path again.

"Go. If you're not back here in an hour, I'll start back to the boat."

"You have your phone?" Dawn asked.

"Yes."

"Okay. Stay here as long as you need to. If you decide to head back, send me a text." She clapped Meg on the shoulder. Part of her realized that was probably inadequate but her emotional inadequacies were the least of her worries at the moment. She turned and ran, as fast as her legs would carry her, down the path.

A couple of hundred yards later, the path widened. She slowed down. When she heard hushed voices ahead, she killed her light. Creeping forward in the dark, one careful footstep after the next, she reached the end of the path. It widened into a circular clearing, choked with weeds. A dilapidated wooden building sat on the other side of the clearing, the lopsided open door spilling sickly yellow light into the area. Mosquitos and other small insects danced in the light.

As Dawn's eyes adjusted to the ambient light, she tried to identify the voices she'd heard. Both men. Most likely Erik and Bill. She scanned the perimeter of the circle and spotted them off to the left of the door, half-hidden behind a small shed. A flare of light as Bill lit a cigarette. Erik gestured wildly. A hard edge crept into their voices. They were arguing about something. Each time Bill took a drag of his smoke, his face was lit in an eerie orange haze. He looked even more haggard than he had in the boat.

She considered going over to help Erik, let him know she was here. But she hung back, biding her time. She'd wait until Bill went inside. More minutes passed. Finally, Bill jutted his chin and in one swift movement, flung his cigarette to the dirt and ground it out with his heel. She shivered. There was something violent and final about it. He turned his back to Erik and strode toward the building. At the door he turned and his gaze swept the area. For a second, she thought he'd seen her. But his eyes landed on Erik. He shook his head, disgusted, then disappeared inside the building.

Dawn took a breath. That part was done at least. She hoped Erik had managed to get more information about where they were holding Timothy. From what she could see, the building was enormous and the door led into only a small part of the abandoned resort.

Before she could move to speak to him, Erik's phone lit up. Worried that he would try to text her, and her phone would ding in the silent clearing, she got ready to move to him. But once he checked the screen, he shoved his cell back into his pocket.

Then he walked across the clearing and disappeared through the same door as Bill.

CHAPTER THIRTY-FOUR

In horror, Dawn watched Erik cross the clearing and walk through the door. *What?* Her mouth dropped open. Why hadn't he texted her the location? He was supposed to be their forward scout. Did he think he could do this on his own?

She sucked in a breath, filling her lungs, then let it out slowly. Now what? Follow him? She needed to wait for Meg. She couldn't just leave her out there in the night to fend for herself. Easing back into a darker area, she turned her back to the door to shield the light from her phone and muted it. Then she texted Meg: *Coming?*

Better. On my way.

She'd have to wait. It would give her time to formulate a plan. She wished she'd been close enough to overhear what Erik and Bill had been arguing about. Bill had been clear that he feared they'd kill him if they found out he led them to the drop point. And of course, he was worried about his brother and sister-in-law. Erik might have pushed that.

Or maybe Erik had just taken the opportunity to follow Bill inside to see if this was where they were holding Timothy?

Dawn turned and secreted herself on the edge of the clearing near the end of the path. For now, she'd have to wait. It seemed like all she'd done all day was hurry up and wait.

Ten long minutes passed, Dawn agitated and burning with impatience, before Erik came through the door, the yellow light a halo around his tall, lean frame. He stood in the opening and scanned the perimeter of the jungle. His gaze dropped to his phone and he moved out from the doorway into the clearing, his eyes not leaving the screen. Moments later, he strode through the weeds to the end of the pathway and stepped into the darkness, barely two yards from where she stood.

She hissed. He turned toward her. "Here," she said.

"What are you doing here? I was coming out to text you."

"We followed. I couldn't stay still any longer."

"Where's Meg?"

"She hurt her foot. I had to leave her behind."

"Left her where?"

"She's on her way. What the hell happened with Bill? I saw you arguing, what was that all about? And where is Timothy?"

He held up a hand. "One question at a time. Come on, let's move farther away." He grabbed her wrist and guided her several yards down the path.

"You saw me arguing with Bill? Why didn't you let me know you were here?"

She shrugged. "I was waiting for him to go inside. I didn't think you'd follow him in there."

"I wanted to see where he was going. I have no idea how big this old place is."

"And?"

"I lost him after a couple of turns. It's a warren of hallways and small rooms. I didn't want him to see the light so I came back out to text you. What's that?" He put a finger to his lips and motioned to the path.

A light bobbed unevenly over the ground. A heavy huffing sound followed. It was Meg. When her light reached their legs, she looked up and continued to hobble toward them.

"Turn the light off," Dawn said.

Meg killed her light and stumbled into Erik. He caught her and held her steady until she regained her balance. She breathed heavily. In the weak light, her face glimmered with perspiration. "Sorry," she said.

"I'm just glad you made it," Dawn said. "How's your foot?"

"Not as bad as I thought," she said. "But I'm not moving very fast."

"No shit, Batman," Erik said.

Meg smiled. "Sorry."

"Stop apologizing," Dawn said. "Lean on me. Erik and I are just formulating a plan to get inside and find Timothy."

"We don't know where he is yet?"

"No. Bill is already inside but Erik lost him."

"Okay." Meg leaned heavily on Dawn, breathless from her trek down the path.

"Maybe you can stay here. Be a look out."

"I'm up to it," Meg said.

"I don't know. We need to be able to move quickly once we're in there."

"I'm up to it," Meg repeated. "I made it this far, didn't I?"

"Yes, and we could hear you coming like a freight train."

"Fine. I'll stay out here."

"I think that's too dangerous," Erik said. "It's better she's with us than left to defend herself out here. We don't know who else is around, or how many are here. I say we all stay together."

Dawn assessed Meg. She would slow them down, no question. But Erik had a point and she couldn't leave her on her own. "Good. So let's go." She looped her arm around Meg's back but Meg shook her off.

"I'm fine," she said. "I can do it myself."

"Just until we're across the clearing," she said. "It's a tangled mess of weeds and we'll be exposed in the light. Let us support you until we get inside out of sight."

CHAPTER THIRTY-FIVE

DAWN WATCHED THE GROUND IN FRONT OF HER FEET AS THEY stumbled together across the clearing. With Eric on one side and Dawn on the other, they had Meg lifted almost off the ground. It was cumbersome, but they moved quickly and quietly toward the light spilling out of the building. As they closed the distance, she kept checking the door, expecting someone else to come through it.

No one did. She let out a breath as they edged into the doorway and out of the open clearing. They were in a narrow hallway. Dank air stung her nostrils. Old posters tacked to the wall, hung down in strips of paper ribbons. This must have been a service entrance. To her immediate right was a small room, probably an office.

They released Meg. She leaned against the wall. The silence was oppressive except for the constant drip of water nearby.

"How far in did you get?" Dawn asked Erik.

"Not far." He waved his arm toward the inner darkness. "It's a maze of hallways. I think we're in the old kitchen and dining area."

"Wait, you said earlier that you lost Bill."

"Right, after a couple of turns. It was too risky to use my light."

Dawn pondered this for a few seconds. "So Bill seemed to know where he was going?"

Erik shrugged. "I guess. I suppose he was here earlier. He probably left from here, is what I mean. Don't you think?"

She pursed her lips. "Maybe." She turned her attention to Meg. "Are you okay to go on?"

"Yes," Meg said, her eyes narrowed and her face scrunched up.

"How much pain are you in?"

"It hurts, but I'm fine."

"She has to come with us," Erik said. "We can't just leave her here."

"Agreed. Let's get moving."

Erik led the way. Dawn followed and Meg limped behind. At the first intersection of hallways, Erik turned right. At the next intersection, he turned left. All around them, the walls pressed in, and the sound of dripping water. Black mold mottled the surfaces, below their feet the floor was slick. Each small sound echoed and bounced, strangely buffered by the dampness.

At the third intersection, he stopped. "This is where I lost him." The hallway opened into three other hallways. One straight ahead. One to the left, the other to the right. "I think there may be a dining room or banquet room up ahead."

"We can split up," Meg said.

They both looked at her.

"Three of us. Three hallways."

Dawn and Erik shook their heads at the same time. "You're not going on your own," Dawn said. "You can't react fast enough with your leg messed up."

"She's right," Erik said. "Why doesn't she come with me? We'll go left, you go right."

Dawn peered into the inky darkness.

"Why not forward?"

"Because I know for sure Bill didn't go straight. I would have seen him if he'd been right in front of me."

She took a breath.

"Unless you have a better idea," Erik added.

She didn't. "Okay. Let's have a backup plan in case things go sideways."

CHAPTER THIRTY-SIX

Dawn watched Erik and Meg move down the hallway. Each shuffle and bump echoed loudly in her ears. She flexed her hands, shook out some of her building tension, and started down the corridor to the right. She cloaked the flashlight and shined only a narrow beam directly below her feet. It was slow going. Multiple doors ran down the right side of the hall, most hanging lopsided within the frames, the wood swollen and twisted. At each one, she stopped and pressed her ear up against the door. No Timothy.

Moving cautiously forward, she reached a large double door on the left. She peered through the crack between the two doors. Darkness and silence within. Taking a minute, she checked her phone for notifications. No word from Erik. She continued on. More doors on the left, numerous small rooms and offices. In front of one, someone had scuffed up the mildew. She leaned in, listening. Again nothing. Dreading that it may creak, she carefully turned the knob. It turned easily. The door had been left unlocked. She pushed inward but it didn't yield. Putting her shoulder against it, she pushed, the swollen wood scraping against the floor beneath it.

She held her breath. Waited. Still nothing. She pushed it open another few inches, enough to shine her light inside. Rusted barrels were stacked to the ceiling against one wall. Wedging the door open a bit more, she stuck her head in. Newer wooden crates were piled against the back wall. There were no identifying marks on the crates.

She pushed the door open another few inches and slid sideways through the narrow opening. The floor beneath her feet had grooves through the mold where things had been dragged around. The smell of fresh wood mingled with the damp. The crates were roughhewn, the boards splintered and bound together at the corners with large staples. Stepping forward, she pointed her light in through one of the cracks. Straw. Packing material for whatever was inside.

She wedged the blade of her knife under the lip of the lid and tried to lever it upward. It protested loudly, the staples squealing. Her chest tightened. She paused and listened.

Her phone, which she'd put down on the crate beside the one she was working on, vibrated. Her eyes dropped to the notification. A text from Erik: *Trouble.*

Backing slowly out of the room, she pulled the door shut, inch by inch, the wood scraping over the floor like a oncoming freight train. She stood in the hall, pulse racing and listening. Satisfied she hadn't been heard, she hurried back to their meet point.

As she rounded the corner, Erik flicked the light on his phone. He waited in the shadows for her to reach him. He was alone.

"Where's Meg?"

"I don't know. That's the problem. I left her for five minutes to check things out down a long hallway and when I came back she was gone."

"What do you mean she was gone?"

"Gone. Gone. How else could I mean it? One minute she

was there and then she wasn't." Erik glared down at her, his brow furrowed.

"Did you check nearby?"

"I hightailed it the hell out of there," he said. "What's the point in both of us being caught?"

"You think someone grabbed her?"

"I don't know what to think. She couldn't just disappear into thin air."

"Did you try texting her?"

"I wasn't sure if that would be a good idea. If they have her, it might be better for them to think she's alone."

Dawn's heart sank. Now they might have Meg, too? She regretted her decision to bring Meg.

"We'll find her," Dawn said. "Let's retrace your steps."

Erik spun on one heel and strode away. Dawn followed. The left-hand hallway was a mirror image of the one she'd explored on the other side. Multiple doors to the right and, on the left, double doors. She reached out and jabbed Erik on the shoulder. He turned.

"Did you see anything else?"

"Nothing. The hall continues with all these small doors and I think there's a big dining room or banquet hall here." He motioned to the right.

"Right. Same on the other side. Have you heard anything?"

"I heard scraping. Like something grinding across the floor. Sounded like it came from inside."

The sound had carried farther than she thought. She might as well have sent up a flare to let them know they were here. "That was me. I found a room on the other side that's being used. It's full of crates."

"Crates of what?"

She shrugged. "Don't know. I was getting ready to open one when you texted. Let's keep going. Stop when you get to the spot where you left Meg."

Erik continued down the hall. They passed three more double doors. He'd made more headway than she had. But then, she'd been exploring those boxes.

They reached another intersection, a T-section. The hall went left and right. "I think this is the end of the banquet room," Erik said. "This is where I left Meg. I went to the right. She was supposed to stay right here."

Dawn shined her light down the hall to the right, then swiveled and shined it to the left. "Did you look down this hall to the left?"

"I did. This place goes on forever. At the end of that hall, it zigs to the right again."

"Did you check all the doors and little rooms on the way back?" She cast her light up the hallway they'd just come down. "Maybe they grabbed her and stashed her?"

"Of course," he said, a hint of impatience edging his words. "I listened at each one. And I didn't see any evidence of the doors being opened recently."

Dawn flipped her phone over. "I'll text her. If she's nearby, we'll hear it."

"Bad idea," Erik said, reaching out to stop her. "We have our phones muted, so no, she won't hear it. If they have her, they could be watching her phone for messages."

He was right. "Damn. What then?"

"We keep going. If they have her, they might be holding her wherever they have Timothy."

She tipped her chin and stepped around him, leading the way this time. "Let's go."

As she slipped past him, a blood curdling scream shredded the silence.

CHAPTER THIRTY-SEVEN

THE SCREAM ECHOED THROUGH THE LONG HALLWAY. DAWN took off on a tear, dashing toward the noise. Behind her, Erik's footsteps followed. Moments later they reached another intersection. Straight on or to the left. She calculated straight on would take them to the far corner of the banquet room and back up the hallway where she'd found the crates. The scream had come from farther away, she was almost certain of it. She stepped to the nearest set of double doors and put her eye up to the crack. No light. No noise. Nobody inside. She veered down the left hallway, Erik on her heels.

Meg screamed again. The shrill panic of it sent a chill down Dawn's spine. She quickened her pace, not caring if she was heard. Behind her, Erik hissed for her attention. She ignored him and kept going. His hand shot out and grabbed her shoulder as he hissed again.

She stumbled, thrown off balance, his fingers digging into her collar bone. His other hand came up to steady her. She fell back against his chest. He wrapped his arms around her in a bear hug.

Pushing his arms down, she broke his hold on her and

stepped out of his embrace. "What the hell, Erik?" Twisting on the ball of her foot, she turned to face him.

He held his finger up to his lip. "Listen," he mouthed and pointed to his ear.

In the claustrophobic confines of the hallway, all she could hear was her heart pounding and Erik breathing. She willed her pulse to slow. In the background, she heard men's voices. The voice from the phone. Miguel's voice. And Jose.

"There's three of them," she said.

"At least three," Erik said. "There may be more."

"Bill never came out. They probably have him, too."

Erik shrugged. "Bill's not our problem."

"That's harsh."

Erik shrugged again. "Look, it sounds like they're in the next banquet room. Since we're outnumbered, why don't I go around so we can come in from both sides? It will give us an element of surprise."

"It's risky to split up. We already lost Meg."

"No guts, no glory." He attempted a grin, only one side of his mouth cooperating.

"Fine, but hurry. We need to get to Meg. I'll be in place by the time you're over there."

"I'll wait for you to enter and come in right away. I'll text you when I'm in place."

"Good," she said, reaching out to push him. "Go!"

As he turned away, another scream tore through the air.

Dawn's whole body tensed. She tried to calculate how long it would take Erik to get in place. It didn't matter. He'd text her. She needed to move. If she had to go in alone, she would. She knew how cruel Miguel could be. She took off down the hall-way, shining her light at her feet.

Partway down, she glimpsed a bit of red on the floor. It lay just outside the small circle of light and she almost missed it. She backed up. A red hair elastic. One of Meg's. As she bent to pick it up, she heard a tapping behind her. She twisted. There was no one. The tapping continued. She backed up slowly, the noise growing louder. Two rooms back on the right, she saw that the entrance had been used recently.

Reaching to her back, she pulled her gun. She tapped twice at the door. Two taps came back. She leaned into the door, her ear flattened against the wood. Something muffled, a cry perhaps. With a light touch, she tried the door knob. Like the other door, it was unlocked. She pushed slowly inward, then shined the light inside. The tapping came again.

She edged the door wider and illuminated a foot, two feet, two legs tightly bound. She stuck her gun in the opening and pushed wider, ready to jump back if necessary. The pulse in her neck thumped out of control, competing with the tapping.

Sucking in a deep breath, she pushed the door wider and stepped inside. Quickly she scanned the small space, shining the light with her left hand, aiming the gun with her right.

She couldn't believe her eyes. She choked and no words would come.

Liquid heat raced through her body.

She stood rooted to the spot, staring. In shock.

CHAPTER THIRTY-EIGHT

Dawn clamped down hard and bit the inside of her cheek, an old trick from her boxing days, to snap her back into the present. It worked. She closed the door of the tiny room behind her. Timothy sprawled on the floor in front of her. The photographs hadn't done justice to the beatings they'd given him. His face was a pulpy mess. His head lolled crookedly to the side. He peered up at her through slit eyes. He was gagged, the blood-soaked cloth bit into his mouth.

Beside him, Meg tried to speak from behind her gag. Dawn knelt beside her and removed the filthy kerchief. Meg gulped in deep breaths. Dawn held a finger to her lips and turned to remove Timothy's gag.

Working quietly, she untied Meg's hands. While Meg worked on the ropes around her ankles, Dawn slipped a blade through the zip tie binding his hands. Timothy was barely conscious.

"How long have you been here?" she asked Meg, her voice barely a whisper.

"I don't know." She knelt, spit on a piece of her shirt, and attempted to clean some of the caked blood from Timothy's eyes. "Erik asked me to wait and the next thing I knew, someone knocked me on the head."

"Who hit you?"

"I didn't see them. I blacked out. When I came to I was here. I heard someone in the hallway, I took a chance it was you, and started tapping with my foot." Her lip trembled and a tear slid down her cheek. Dawn shined the light into her face. There was a nasty gash near her temple and it was already rising into a sizable bump.

Timothy groaned and tried to reach for Dawn. A scorpion skittered up his pant leg and Dawn flicked it off.

"Meg, rub his wrists and try to get some circulation back into his hands." Timothy's arms were blemished with deep grooves and purple welts where the zip ties had dug cruelly into his flesh.

"Water," Timothy croaked.

Dawn shined the light through the small space. "There's no water. We have to get you out of here."

"There's four of them," he said. "Maybe more."

"How did you get here? All we've seen is a rowboat."

"Speedboat. There's a pier across the island." He coughed.

Dawn held a finger to her lips. "Can you guide us back?"

"I think so."

"They dropped you off? Were there other boats?"

"I think so, yeah."

"We'll have to leave that way. Back to the Papa Joe is too far and we'll never outrun them in a rowboat and the Papa Joe."

She turned to Meg. "We need to get you guys out of here. Can you stand? I need help with Timothy." She extended her hand and pulled Meg upright.

Meg reached out and grabbed a shelf, weaving. "I'm woozy," she said.

"They hit you hard," Dawn said. "We'll keep an eye to make

sure you're not concussed. Timothy, too." She slanted a look at him and cursed under her breath. "Let's get the hell out of here."

Together, she and Meg got Timothy to his feet. His limbs were bruised but not broken. "I don't have any feeling in my legs," he said.

"It'll come back. Meg, come to this side so your good leg bears the most weight."

Once Dawn had him supported between the two of them, she opened the door, inch by inch. "We need to move as quickly as possible. And stay quiet."

She paused in the doorway. Erik. Could she leave him behind? Timothy choked, a feeble sound, and she made her decision. Get him and Meg out. She'd come back for Erik.

They made their way slowly down the hallway. At each intersection, Dawn tried to retrace her steps in reverse. If she made a wrong turn, they'd lose precious time. Any minute now Erik would be texting that he was in place. In fact, he should have already texted. She calculated they were two thirds of the way to the end of the last banquet hall, almost to the exit, when the notification slid onto the screen of her phone: *In place.*

She ignored it and kept pushing for the door. Timothy was dead weight. He hung between them like a limp scarecrow, his legs like jelly, his feet slipping awkwardly along the floor. Thank heavens he wasn't that big to begin with. Meg limped heavily, lurching to the side with each stride forward, throwing the weight off center. Dawn bore the brunt and kept them moving forward. Five more minutes and they would be outside.

A second notification from Erik: *Ready?*

Three more minutes and they'd reach the door.

Meg paused, panting. "I'm not sure I can keep going."

"We're almost there," Dawn said. "Keep going."

"I can't do it," she said.

"You can," Dawn said. "And you will. You think these assholes won't kill us all?"

They lurched through the door into the clearing. Thirty yards away lay the safety of darkness. It may as well have been a football field. As they cleared the door, the night was split again by the sound of a woman screaming.

CHAPTER THIRTY-NINE

THE BLOOD CURDLING SCREAM REVERBERATED THROUGH THE night. All three stopped in their tracks, frozen in the weak yellow light spilling out into the yard, their shadows thrown long and narrow across the weeds.

"What the hell was that?" Meg said.

"I don't know," Dawn said, urging them forward. "Keep going, we need to get to the trees. Earlier I thought it was you.

"Timothy, do you know if they have anyone else here?"

"Don't know." He choked and spat out blood.

"Save your energy, we'll talk later." Dawn kept the small group moving forward, her eye fixed on where the halo of light ended, where the jungle darkened, and where there might be at least the illusion of temporary safety. She had to respond to Erik. He was going to get antsy and come looking for her. Which could be a good thing. He was smart, maybe he'd figure it out and retrace their path until he found her.

Meg tripped, her toe caught in the weeds. As she went down, Timothy went with her. Dawn's arm was wrenched almost out of her socket as she struggled to keep them upright.

Unable to hold them, she let them go, succeeding only in lessening the blow as they hit the ground.

Meg started to sob. Timothy threw up again.

"Get up," Dawn said, clawing at Meg's arm. "Come on, we can't stay here in the light."

She forced her shoulder under Timothy's arm pit, braced herself, and pushed with her knees until she had him almost upright. Then she hoisted him over her shoulder in a fireman's carry and staggered toward the trees.

"Dawn," Meg said.

"Crawl if you have to." Dawn kept going, the darkness only yards away.

Sobbing, on all fours, Meg followed.

Finally, as she carried Timothy farther into the jungle, Dawn let out a breath. She set his bruised and battered body to the ground and returned to Meg. She pulled her to her feet and helped her to Timothy's side.

Another scream wrenched through the night. Damn it.

"I'm going to have to go back," she said.

Meg clutched at her arm. "You can't. We need to get off this island. What about Timothy?"

"I can't leave that woman behind. Plus, Erik." She pulled out her phone. Another notification from Erik. "I need to let him know I'm on my way."

"Dawn, it may have been Erik who knocked me out."

Dawn shook her head. "No. He's been with us from the beginning."

"There was nobody else around."

"How would Erik even know where to put you? He was helping us look for Timothy." Dawn leaned over, her hands on her knees, panting. Timothy was light enough but she'd carried him a long distance.

"Is he waiting for you now?"

"Yeah, I need to text him."

"Wait," Meg said. "Please think it through. Put him off for a few minutes, give us time to think."

Dawn sent off a quick text: *5 minutes.*

She changed tack. "Timothy, I overheard Miguel on one of the calls. He's in there, right?"

"Yeah, him and Jose."

"And who was making the calls?"

"I never saw his face," Timothy said. "Earlier in the day they had me blindfolded. Later, he always kept his back to me. I tried to warn you. Did you find my gun?"

"I did. I knew it was some kind of message, but—"

"It's all a sham. They don't want the money. It's all a trap to lure you here."

"But why?" Meg asked.

"I'm the sole witness." Dawn's voice was flat as Timothy confirmed what she'd suspected. "Without me they have no case against the bastards who killed Joe."

"Dawn, you can't go back in. Whether Erik is with us, or with them, you can't go back."

As if on cue, the woman's scream cut through the night again.

"You'll have to take him to the dock," Dawn said.

Meg shook her head. "It's too dangerous. Don't go back. How much more information do you need?"

"Look, that could be your sister in there. Or your cousin, or your mother. I'm going back. Can you manage Timothy or not?"

Meg scrambled to her feet and threw her arms around Dawn's neck. "I can. Don't get yourself killed."

Surprised by Meg's show of emotion, Dawn stepped back. She needed to focus. She couldn't afford to be soft.

"I won't. I'll see you at the dock."

CHAPTER FORTY

DAWN RETRACED HER STEPS ALONG THE HALLWAY, RACING back toward the second banquet room, back to where the screams were coming from. She hoped Meg could manage with Timothy. She should have told them to get in a boat and keep going once they got to the pier. There was no reason for them to risk themselves more. Her fault. All of this was her fault. They didn't want Timothy. They didn't want money. They only wanted her.

She'd known it. When they made her go to the reef where Joe had died, she'd suspected. When they sent her back to the little cove, her suspicions had been confirmed. At that moment, she should have left Erik and Meg behind somewhere. Dropped them off on an island and come on her own. What the hell had she been thinking?

She slowed as she drew closer to the room where the screams were coming from. A narrow shaft of light slanted out through the double doors. She knew that on the opposite side of the room, on the double doors that mirrored hers, Erik was in place, ready for them to burst in.

She stilled herself and peered in through the crack in the doors. Three men sat in a circle. She recognized Miguel's profile. She'd recognize him anywhere. Jose was sitting with his face square on to her. The third man had his back to her. They hunched around a small tablet, watching something.

"Play it again," the man said.

Jose leaned forward and pressed a button. The woman's scream filled the room.

"Oh, that's so good. It sounds like it's happening right here," Miguel said.

"I know, right?" Jose beamed in the flickering light.

"You're sure she'll come for that?" It was the man's voice from the phone.

"She'll come," Miguel said. "She has this ingrained sense of right and wrong. No way she's leaving here if she thinks there's somebody in trouble."

Dawn tiptoed back from the door. *A recording.*

Well, they were right. The screams had brought her back in here. But now she knew what they were up to and could get the hell out of here.

A notification flashed on her phone: *Let's go.*

Erik was in place. If Meg was right, she couldn't afford to let him know she suspected him. But if Meg was wrong, she couldn't live with herself if she left him behind.

She had an idea.

She responded: *I can't see much. Who is the guy with his back to me?*

Don't know him.

Can you see Bill?

He's tied up against the wall, just inside the door where you are.

Dawn's finger hovered over the keypad. She took a breath and typed: *What about Meg and Timothy?*

They're tied up beside Bill.

Dawn stared at the screen for ten seconds, disappointment squeezing her chest.

She texted back: *Loading my gun. Ready in 5.*

Then she turned and ran for the exit, her legs pumping as she pushed herself faster and faster.

CHAPTER FORTY-ONE

E RIK SHIFTED HIS WEIGHT TO HIS OTHER LEG. I T WAS TAKING much too long for Dawn to get ready. What the hell was holding her up? He flicked open the app on his phone and grunted with displeasure. Drawing his gun, he stepped through the double doors.

"Whoa," Miguel said, leaping to his feet. "What the hell are you doing here?"

"She's already gone outside." Erik stalked across the open room to where the men were gathered.

"What?" Miguel jammed his hands on his hips.

The man Erik didn't know as well, the one whose name was never spoken, stared at Miguel. "You said she'd come for the screams. You guaranteed it. Guess you don't know shit." He turned his eagle gaze on Erik. Erik squirmed like a worm about to be skewered by a hook. "And you, how do you know she's outside? You were supposed to get her here."

Erik tucked his gun back into his waistband and waved his cell in the air. "I synced our phones earlier. I have an app that tracks her location."

"Well, why the hell weren't you tracking her location earlier?"

"I was. That's how I knew she was here earlier. It's why I went outside."

"That doesn't help us now. Why didn't you know where she was all the time?" The man's translucent eyes sparked in the candlelight.

"I did. She was here."

"You just said she's not here."

"Right. Now she's gone."

The man spat on the ground, disgusted. "Gone where? Where the hell is she?"

"She's heading out of the building. I'll go after her." Erik turned back to the door.

"Jose, go with him," the man said.

Erik turned back. "No. It'll tip her off. She still thinks I'm on her side. I'll go on my own."

———

The man stood, smoothing the creases in his tan linen trousers. "Miguel, go and check on our guests. Jose, you follow that asshole. I want you to keep him in your sights at all times."

The men left the room and he paced to the cooler and cracked open a cold beer. He tipped it to his lips and swallowed. Footsteps pounded down the hall. Miguel burst through the door, his face red with exertion. "They're gone."

Of course they were.

He threw the bottle against the wall. It smashed into jagged pieces, beer spraying everywhere.

Idiots. He was plagued with idiots all around him.

"Don't just stand there," he said. "Go after them."

CHAPTER FORTY-TWO

Dawn tore along the path toward the west side of the island. Her thighs burned and her heart pounded in her chest like a jackhammer. Each breath she drew burned like live flame. She ignored it and kept pushing forward.

She kept her light on the uneven path in front of her, leaping over vines and exposed roots. Bits of leaves and vine littered the path. Like the trail they'd come in on, the jungle encroaching on this path had been recently trimmed back with a machete. The ground was slick. The night was inky black. No moon blemished the sky. Large leaves slapped against her face and her raised arm as she barreled down the path. Nocturnal critters chirped and burped in the jungle around her. A large scorpion skittered across the path.

Finally, she burst through the end of the trail onto a pebble beach. A light flared to her left. She headed toward the dock at the far north end of the beach.

She sprinted onto the weathered dock, the wood rotted and splintered. Some boards missing, others broken. Huffing with exertion, she slowed her pace and picked her way down the precarious dock, her eyes glued to the uneven and shifting surface. Meg and Timothy sat on a jet ski.

"There's one for you," Meg said. "The key is in it."

"Why not the boat?"

"We couldn't find the key."

Dawn hesitated. Timothy listed to the side, his arm trailing down along the running board. Timothy should come with her, she was stronger. But it put him in more danger. Better they have the chance to get away without her. "Hang on," she said. She dug under the seat and pulled out a bungee cord. "Let me secure Timothy with this. If he passes out, he'll fall off."

She leaned over, wrapped the bungee around Timothy and secured it to the grip bar at the back. Standing back, she surveyed her work. It made things worse. Now he had to put tension on the cord in order to hang onto Meg.

"Where's Erik?" Meg asked.

"You were right. He's a plant." Dawn looked at Meg. "I think we need to secure Timothy to you. Are you strong enough for that?"

"I'm fine," Timothy mumbled.

"Do it," Meg said."Does he know you found him out?"

"I'm not sure. But it won't take them long to figure it out." Dawn wrapped the bungee cord around Timothy's back, then snapped the hooks into place around Meg's rib cage. "Is that digging into you?" Meg adjusted the hooks away from her body.

"You go, Meg. I'll be right behind you."

"Go where? What's our plan?"

"Head north along the shoreline. If you reach the end of the island before I catch up with you, wait for me there." She toed the front of the jet ski and pushed them off.

Meg turned on the engine and idled in reverse away from the dock. Dawn wished she had a life jacket for Timothy. If he went overboard in his state, it would be disastrous. Meg was a strong swimmer but with her injured leg any time in the water would be a struggle. Going forward, there was little room for error.

Dawn climbed aboard the other machine and killed her light. She turned the ignition. It clicked but didn't start.

"Dawn, they're coming."

CHAPTER FORTY-THREE

Looking to shore, Dawn spotted light filtering through the dense jungle. She turned the key in the ignition again. Nothing.

In the background, she heard Meg shut down her engine. Damn it, she wanted them already gone. Now she had Timothy and Meg to worry about. Having people in her life just created more problems.

The light rapidly closed the distance between them. Pebbles crunched underfoot as the man raced across the beach. Then a heavy footfall on the small dock. He tripped and stumbled on the rough boards but righted himself. Dawn sprang off the machine and braced her legs against the jarring movement of the swaying dock. She shined her light into Erik's face.

"Stay right there," she said.

"Hey." He threw up his hand to shield his eyes, put his light down. "I've been looking all over for you. I thought we were getting Timothy and Meg before leaving."

Dawn scoffed. "Come on, Erik, don't be an asshole. You think I don't know?" He reached for his gun, but she was faster.

She drew and aimed at his chest. "Drop that and kick it over here."

"I'm on your side."

"Like hell you are. Are you deaf? I'm sure you just heard Meg yell to me." Erik's eyes narrowed. She raised her arm higher, aimed at his face. "For a bright guy, you seem to be missing a lot. Drop your weapon. Kick it over here."

Erik sneered and threw his gun on the dock. He toed it forward. It skipped and landed mid-way between them. Without taking her eyes off him, Dawn edged forward and dragged it backward with her foot.

"How long have you known?" Erik asked.

"We're sharing secrets now, are we?" Dawn shook her head. Erik's betrayal cut deep. "How could you get involved with Miguel and Jose? Knowing what they're capable of?"

Erik shrugged. "Money talks."

"Money," she scoffed. "Timothy's life? Meg's? Mine? You sold your soul to the devil. I hope karma bites you in the ass." She backed toward the jet ski. "We're leaving. You're going to turn around and walk toward shore."

"I'm not turning my back on you."

"Unlike you, I won't shoot you in the back. What kind of girl do you think I am?"

"The kind who needs to be taught a lesson." Jose's voice came from the beach, to the left of the dock. "Put the gun down, Dawn."

"No." Dawn kept her weapon aimed at Erik. Erik started to back slowly down the dock.

"I won't tell you again," Jose said. He shined a light at Dawn's face. She squinted into the light, keeping her focus squarely on Erik. He continued to edge backward toward the beach. The dock rocked unsteadily beneath their feet.

A shot rang out from somewhere behind her. Who was firing? Meg had a weapon?

On the shore, Jose cursed and fired wildly back into the void of dark ocean. Dawn shined her light on Jose and took a shot. He screamed and went down.

"Dawn, let's get the hell out of here," Meg shouted. She fired up the jet ski and circled in toward the dock.

Erik yelled, a guttural sound that came up from his belly, and rushed Dawn. She braced herself and aimed squarely at his head. Erik froze. Meg rode up closer and shined her light on him.

"One step further and I will shoot you," Dawn said.

"Dawn, there's more lights coming. We need to go."

Dawn edged toward the jet ski, keeping her weapon aimed at Erik.

"Hurry," Meg said.

Erik sneered at Dawn as she climbed onto the machine. She turned the key. This time the engine roared to life.

Erik stepped forward, closing the distance between them. She pushed off from the dock. He laughed. "You can run but we're gonna find you."

Something inside Dawn snapped. "Yeah, I've heard that before," she said. "Try something more original next time."

She pulled the trigger and took a kill shot. Surprise flared in Erik's eyes. The impact of the bullet forced him backward. As he crashed to the dock, Dawn turned the machine and opened the throttle to full speed.

CHAPTER FORTY-FOUR

Dawn gunned the jet ski away from the dock, following in Meg's wake. She glanced back toward the dock, the light she'd seen now on the beach. It wouldn't be long until they followed. She should have cut the gas line in the speedboat. What the hell had she been thinking?

When would she have done that? When Erik was planning to kill her or when Jose was aiming at her head? With a bit of luck, they wouldn't find the keys either or their head start would give them a slight advantage.

A flash of lightning lit up the sky. She knew a long day of heat could bring on this kind of weather. She hoped it was only heat lightning. Her jet ski skimmed over the top of the waves. She was lighter than Meg and Timothy and would overtake them in a few minutes. Lightning flashed again, illuminating a rocky point. She turned outward and opened the throttle. She passed Meg on the outside and waved her onward.

They ate up the miles northward along the shoreline. The water grew choppier, more lightning flashed. Each time it gave her night blindness. She blinked rapidly, trying to refocus to the night.

The darkness on the water was so complete, she moved deeper into the open channel each time she caught a glimpse of the rocky shoreline. There was no way they'd see anything in the water before they hit it.

A boom of thunder momentarily drowned out the whine of the engine. The water grew choppier, the small craft bumping over the waves. On this side of the island, there was no shelter. The next flash of lightning lit up the western horizon and revealed banks of thunderheads crowding the sky. She counted off until the next roll of thunder. They didn't have long before the storm was upon them.

When the lightning flashed again, she scanned the shoreline for a small cove, a stretch of beach, anywhere they could pull in and get off the water. There was nothing, the coastline jagged and inhospitable. They'd crash against the rocks and be stranded.

Large drops of rain hit her head, splashed against her face. She peered into the dark and pushed the jet ski harder. She hoped Meg and Timothy weren't far behind.

Lightning flashed above, followed quickly by a crash of thunder. This time, she could see the storm rolling at them from the west. A solid wall of rain. Wind licked at the little craft. She struggled to keep it moving forward in a straight line. As the waves got larger, she sought out the troughs. The next slash of lightning illuminated the point at the end of the island. She slowed and turned to wait for Meg, struggling to keep her bow headed into the waves.

Meg idled up beside her, shielding her eyes, Timothy slumped against her back, his arms around her waist. "We need to get off the water," she yelled. The wind whipped at her words. "Let's head back down the other side. Maybe there's more shelter."

"We can't go backwards," Dawn said.

"We're completely exposed out here. They won't be far

behind us. They'll pick us off like shore-birds. Let's head back to your boat. At least we'll have shelter and more ammunition."

"Where did you get the gun?" Dawn asked.

"In the speedboat when I was looking for the keys."

"There's probably someone watching the Papa Joe. We'll have to keep going."

"In this? This storm is just getting warmed up."

"The shoreline here is too rocky to land. There's another island not much farther north. Remember?"

"We're gonna get slammed going across that narrow channel. Are you sure about this?"

"I don't see another way. We'll cross the channel and go down the lea side of the other island. Find a place to beach. Hide or sink the jet skis and get a rescue call out to the Coast Guard."

Lightning lit up Meg's face. Her eyes were wide and she shook her head. "Crossing that channel's a bad idea."

"Do you have a better one? If we round this point and get back on this island, we might as well sign our own death warrants."

"I don't want to die today," Meg yelled.

Timothy lifted his head and fixed a glassy stare at Dawn. "Get us home, Dawn."

"That's the plan," Dawn said. Timothy faded back onto Meg's shoulder.

"Go," Dawn said. "I'll stay behind you. If we get separated, you beach at the first safe place you find."

Rain lashed down, streaming down Meg's face. She shielded her eyes and pointed to the south. "I see running lights."

Dawn turned and squinted into the storm. Lights bumped over the waves. They were still a distance off, but it wouldn't take long for them to reach them.

"Go," she said, jutting her head northward. "I'll see you on shore."

CHAPTER FORTY-FIVE

WHITE CAPS LICKED AT THE BOW OF THE LITTLE CRAFT AS Dawn crashed over the waves, her hands and arms bearing the brunt each time the machine slammed back down onto the water. The injury in her wrist flared up, shooting flames of pain up her arm.

She held back on the accelerator, staying behind Timothy and Meg. Meg struggled to remain on course. They passed the northern point of the island, lumbering into the open channel. The other island only a mile away. Good news, bad news. The channel between them churned unpredictably, crashed against rocky points. Meg fought against the wind and currents, got bogged down in the troughs, then would fight up over the waves again.

Dawn glanced back over her shoulder. The boat following not more than half a mile behind them. She urged Meg forward. *Come on.*

Rain streamed over her. Her clothing clung to her body. She ignored the discomfort, kept her eye on Meg and Timothy. From behind her came the whine of the approaching boat. It wouldn't be long. Meg was a quarter of the way across the chan-nel, the ocean tossing jet ski around like a child's toy. A couple of times, Dawn was sure they'd flip.

Each time they rode the trough to the bottom, she lost sight of them.Held her breath waiting for them to come back up. A rogue wave hit her side on, rolling the jet ski and knocking the breath out of her. She tightened her grip, rolled her weight to the opposite side. She scanned the water ahead of her but couldn't find Meg.

The speedboat roared up on her port side. Two figures on board that she could make out. It sped past her, bouncing wildly over the white caps, then hit the trough and sank almost out of her sight. And there. Meg and Timothy surfaced just to her right. The boat rode the wave again, only ten yards out from Meg and Timothy, throwing more waves and wake toward them. The passenger in the boat fixed a spotlight on Meg and fired into the night, the sound of the shot almost lost under the constant squeal of the wind. Meg ducked, throwing her body low below the windshield. Timothy's body crashed to the side as the bullet slammed into him.

Meg disappeared again. The boat sped past them and turned to come up along the other side. At the last minute, it turned sharply away from a span of jagged rocks.

Dawn reached for her gun, but grabbed at the handles when the jet ski lurched to the side. She couldn't maintain the machine with only one hand on the controls. The waves crashed and churned around her. To her right, the rocks. To her left, somewhere, Meg and Timothy. The speedboat was making another tight loop.

Meg surged up over a wave, the jet ski coming out of the water. She crashed back down. A sickening sound filled the air as the hull hit the rocks. Meg and Timothy were thrown off into the water. Dawn steered toward them, yelling Meg's name.

Before she could close the distance between them, the speedboat cut her off. The passenger fired several shots into the water where she'd last seen Meg. Then the boat headed straight for her.

CHAPTER FORTY-SIX

"Get closer."

Miguel pushed the boat against the waves, the bow dropping heavily against each whitecap. "I'm doing what I can here. Why don't you just shoot her? Let's get this over with."

"I want her alive." The caller cuffed Miguel up against the side of his head. "Are you that stupid? If I wanted her dead, she'd already be dead."

"She killed my best friend."

The other man grunted. "Erik? He messed up. He deserved what he got."

"No, we just hired him the other day," Miguel said, steering the boat closer to the jet ski. "I meant Jose."

"He didn't look that bad," the other man said. "Probably only mostly dead."

Miguel grunted and shielded his face against the rain. "How close do you need me to get?" They were still yards away from Dawn and the jet ski.

"Close enough to grab her."

"How the hell are we going to do that in this weather? It's too choppy."

"Get closer." He who would not be named stepped away, pulled a boat hook from the stern, and extended it to its full length. "We'll knock her off the damn thing and she'll have no choice but to let us bring her in."

CHAPTER FORTY-SEVEN

THE BOW OF THE SPEEDBOAT BORE DOWN ON DAWN. THEY weren't slowing down. There was nowhere for her to go. In desperation, she pulled her gun and aimed at the windshield. Her shot went wild as the jet ski lurched to the side with a rolling wave. She reached for the controls but flailed, her feet sliding beneath her as she tried to plant them on something solid. Lightning split the night revealing a wave of water coming straight for her face. It hit her solidly before she had time to take a breath.

Beneath the waves, the current rolled and dragged Dawn. She fought for control. Below was blackness. Above she could see nothing but the jet ski tumbling down toward her. She pulled hard with her arms, kicking with her legs to get out from under the machine. Her leg scraped against something sharp. Pain seared through her thigh as the jet ski hit the back of her leg and pinned her in place against a rock.

She grabbed an outcrop of rock and tried to pull herself from beneath the machine. The jagged edge of the rock cut deeply into her front thigh. She turned and frantically pushed against the machine with both hands. She didn't have enough leverage.

Her lungs burned. She was running out of the little air she had.

She twisted and kicked at the bottom of the machine with her other leg, trying to force it upward. A slight release. At the same time, she dragged herself forward, cringing against the tear in her leg. She was at once pinned and weightless, terrified and determined not to die. Not here. Not tonight.

With one final kick, she released her thigh and dragged herself forward. The small craft slipped away as she clawed to the surface, her lungs bursting.

Her head broke the surface and she gulped, taking in equal amounts of air and salt water. A wave slammed her face. She took a stroke forward, not sure of her direction, only sure she needed to move.

Something prodded at her shoulder. She reached back, turned to see what it was. The speedboat had hooked her. She fought against it but couldn't release the hook. The man pushed her downward, and she took in more water. Then pulled her up, lifting her partway out of the water. Her head cracked the side of the boat.

A strong arm reached down for her. She pushed it away. The man reached around the front of her neck and she bit at his wrist. He cuffed her against the head, slammed her head into the hull of the boat again. The current dragged her under as the boat listed dangerously above her.

Then the back of her shirt lifted away from her body and, with a strong sucking noise, she was pulled from the water and dragged roughly over the side into the boat.

CHAPTER FORTY-EIGHT

DAWN LANDED FACE DOWN ON THE DECK OF THE SPEEDBOAT, her chin slamming down inches away from a large brown boot. The fall knocked the breath out of her lungs. She struggled for air, gulping like a fish out of water. Her whole body ached like she'd been dragged over a gigantic cheese grater. Her vision faded in and out.

Overhead, the sky lit up with a flash of lightning followed by a deep crack of thunder. She peered up to get a peek of the man in the boots.

Miguel. Water streamed down his face. When he caught her looking, his full lips twisted cruelly. He sneered down at her and placed his boot on her neck. "We meet again," he said.

She coughed and choked on water caught in her throat. She struggled to roll onto her side, clawing at his boot, but he didn't release her.

"Let her be." From somewhere far away, seconds before she choked on her own vomit, she recognized the voice as the one belonging to the caller. Miguel removed his foot and Dawn wrenched to the side, spewing up sea water and bile. Spent, she curled into a semi-fetal position, her cheek resting against the cool, wet surface beneath her.

Her unfocused gaze landed on her leg. A deep gash started below the hem of her shorts, her skin shredded. Pink water rolled down over her knee. Blood blossomed through her shorts higher up her thigh. Seeing the injury made it more real and her leg began to pulse. The salt water drenching her shorts bit cruelly into the open wound. She gnawed the inside of her cheek, determined not to cry out with the pain that screamed through her.

"Want me to tie her up?"

The caller's voice came to her as she drifted in and out of consciousness. "She's not going anywhere. Let's head back."

They were taking her back. Back to what? Part of her didn't care. They might as well kill her now. How could her life be worth living after this? They'd shot Meg and Timothy. She'd done her best to save Timothy. But in the end she'd failed him. Like she'd failed Meg, but for different reasons. She never should have let Meg come along. Never should have exposed her to such danger. She'd known it was risky but she'd been selfish. Weak. Fearful.

She cringed. Meg and Timothy had paid for her stupidity. Her only two friends were now at the bottom of the ocean. Why did death inside on following her around? Everybody that got close to her ended up dying. She was like a disease. Deadly Dawn. That's what they should start calling her.

She rolled onto her back and stared up into the storm, letting the rain hit her full in the face. Maybe the relenting onslaught of water would wash away her sins. For each person who was dead because of her, she counted to a hundred, trying to keep her mind busy and quell the physical pain ravaging her body. First hundred for the boxer. Second hundred for her brother. Third hundred for Joe.

She should have quit there. Joe, who had been more like family than her own blood. Who had reached a hand down for her when she was at her lowest. Who had pulled her up from a slow but certain death through self-destruction.

What did Joe get for all his trouble? A belly full of salt water and plankton.

Like the fourth hundred. And the fifth. Timothy and Meg. Gone now, too.

And this would be her day to die. She could feel it.

Miguel kicked her in the ribs. "Wake up. Time to die."

Was he really quoting *Blade Runner*? She was fading in and out but the toe in her ribs had felt real.

"Leave her," the caller said. He hovered over her, his face in darkness. The illuminated console threw a kaleidoscope of colored light around his head. His voice lowered, he spoke almost as if to himself. "She's not what I was expecting."

See? She'd even let the kidnapper down. She wanted to laugh. Or did she want to cry? She didn't know. What was the appropriate response for dying, she wondered? Was she going to screw that up, too?

"You haven't seen her fight," Miguel said. Or did she imagine that? Maybe this whole thing was a bitter dream and she would wake up in her bunk aboard the Papa Joe.

Her mind drifted. Did her parents ever think of her? Did they wonder where she was? If she was happy? Was she married? Their idea of an idyllic life for her would have been a husband, a gaggle of kids, and a picket fence in the suburbs.

They hated her. They probably wished her dead. Looks like they were going to get their wish. At least she was going to make someone happy.

As she started to fade again, her mother's face leaned in over her, smoothed her forehead, tucked a strand of hair behind her ear.

She'd do anything to turn back time and have her mother's love again.

A single tear rolled down her cheek.

She missed them.

CHAPTER FORTY-NINE

THE WAVES CLOSED OVER MEG'S HEAD, THE SHARP CRACK OF the gunfire echoing in her ears. The water tugged at her, a weight on her back sucking her down. Like a turtle wrong-side up, she flailed but was unable to turn. Down, down she went, aware of the rocks that surrounded her. Then the bungee cord around her chest tightened and dug into her. Timothy!

In the shock of the moment she'd forgotten Timothy lashed to her back. He thrashed, trying to free himself. Meg's fingers found the hooks. She tried to free him but the cable was taut, digging tightly into her. The more Timothy thrashed, the tighter the cable bound them together. The clips carried so much tension she couldn't loosen them. She clawed at the hooks until her fingers bled. Timothy kicked and clawed, his arms windmilling dangerously close to her head.

Forgetting her injured leg, she tried to kick them both up to the surface. If Timothy had air, she might be able to calm him. But it was no good. She had no power in her injured leg. Timothy wrapped his arms tightly around her and squeezed. She dug her thumbs into the inside of his elbows to release herself, punched backward through the water. Completely panicked, Timothy stroked upward with his arms and Meg kicked with her good leg. But they continued to sink like a stone, ripped along with the current.

Her foot hit something solid. A rock? She braced for impact. They hit bottom. For a long, timeless second, they stood, calm and still on the ocean floor. Bubbles breezed past her peripheral vision as Timothy let some of his breath out.

In that moment of calmness, Meg tried again. Pushing, she wedged her right thumb in under the hook, and then her other thumb in under the hook on the other side. Squeezing with all her might, she forced slack into the cord. Every muscle strained and tensed. Her eyes felt like they were going to pop out of her head. Success. The hooks popped open. She pivoted and pushed Timothy free of her. He shot upwards, the bungee floating free. She grabbed the cord, pushed herself off the bottom, and swam for the surface.

Meg burst out of the water and sucked in air.

The waves towered over her head. The sea tossed her mercilessly. She was dangerously close to an outcropping of rock. Treading water, she stroked backwards, keeping an eye on the jagged edges. She did a three-sixty degree turn but Timothy was nowhere to be seen. Or Dawn. Or the damned speed boat that had shot at them.

A wave surged over her. Timothy called her name. She turned toward the sound, swam in that direction. She caught the top of his head bobbing along the crest of a wave. Then he was gone, slammed down into the shallow. She stretched, fighting the force of the water, trying to reach him. He'd been in and out of consciousness the last several hours. There was little chance he was strong enough to fight against this current. If she didn't reach him, she'd lose him for sure.

She rode the crest of a wave. A faint light sparked about fifty yards away. The speedboat. The wind howled around her.

There wasn't a chance in hell they'd hear them. Good, she didn't need more bullets aimed at her head.

"Meg." Timothy yelled again. She swam forward and spotted him again. He was struggling against the current, waves slamming against his face. His eyes were glassy. She was sure he'd pass out again any second.

"Here," she yelled. She forced her tired arms to pull harder and kicked with both feet, ignoring the pain searing up her leg.

He went under. His arms above his head. Then he surfaced.

"Hang on," she said. Five yards. Three. He went under again. This time he didn't come back up. She dove.

Plunging into the darkness, she tried to gauge the distance and waved her arms wildly, hoping to catch some part of him. Her fingers brushed his hair. She clamped on, pulled him closer. Got her forearm under his chin and kicked again for the surface.

Timothy lay limp in her grasp, his body stretched out and tossed about by the waves, his feet drifting downward. She called his name, but he was out. A blessing really. He was easier to manage this way.

Where to go? Lightning flashed above, briefly illuminating the area. High waves crashed against jagged rocks to her right. The rocky shoreline was too far away, they'd never reach it. A clap of thunder followed. She counted between, as she'd done as a child. Anything to still her racing heart, to jam down the panic and horrible tightness in her gut.

She put her back to the shoreline and treaded water, Timothy floating unevenly in her hold. She waited for the next lightning. If they couldn't get ashore here, they'd have to go to the northern island. The light flashed overhead. All she saw to the north was a wall of rain. Wherever the other island was, it was out of their reach. Her heart sank. Boom went the thunder overhead, so loud it set her teeth on edge.

Her injured leg throbbed. Her arm was starting to cramp.

She switched arms, almost fumbled Timothy in the process. She still clenched the bungee cord tight.

The waves continued to push them closer to the rocks. She pushed away again, fighting against the current which ripped through the channel between the two islands.

Wait. Channel. Islands. Rocks. When the lightning flashed the next time, Meg scanned the top of the waves. There. Barely discernible and dancing wildly like a jack-in-the-box on crack. A flashing red navigation buoy. It looked to be fifty yards away.

Meg choked and tears sprang to her eyes. Hope.

Digging deep, she started to swim toward it.

CHAPTER FIFTY

Dawn woke with a start. Water splashed into her face and she spit out salt water. The boat pitched to the side and she tumbled across the deck. Blinded, she gripped the first thing her fingers found.

"Let go," Miguel yelled, wrenching his ankle out of her grasp. She wiped the water from her eyes and looked up. He was leaning into the wind, his knuckles white on the wheel as the small boat tossed about at the mercy of the waves. As the stern lifted and dropped, the engine roared unevenly. Rain sliced against her skin. Several inches of water slushed around the bottom of the boat. There was nowhere to go that wasn't wet.

She crawled toward the opening to the forward cubby. Before she could reach it, Miguel braced his foot across the opening. "Stay."

She backed up, leaned her back against the wall, and shielded her face from the wind and the sting of the rain in her eyes. She wondered where the caller was. Then she saw him huddled on the back bench, gripping a tarp over his head like a hoodie. It whipped wildly in the rain, the bright orange vivid against the gloom of the storm.

Visibility was almost zero. More than a few yards out from the boat all she could see was a wall of rain and water. White-caps curled over the boat. Waves loomed over Miguel's head and hit them broadside, water spilling into the boat, swamping them over the sides. Miguel fought with the wheel to get them righted and headed into the onslaught of the next wave. Zooming down into the trough, she stood and clung to the rail beneath the windshield. The boat shuddered at the bottom and started the climb back up the other side.

"Where is he?" Dawn yelled.

Miguel slanted her a look, his eyes dark as the storm. "Who?"

"Dylan."

The boat rolled into the wave, water spilled in over the port gunwale. "Shut the hell up," he said. "I'm busy. Start bailing this water out of here."

She fumbled along the side, looking for some sort of container. At the stern, the caller hunched further into the tarp and turned away from her. She reached her arm beneath the small space, groping for something to use. Anything. Her fingers brushed against something metal. She pulled out a gallon-sized can and started scraping it along the deck, bailing the water out of the bottom and flinging it over the side. Half of what she sent into the wind came straight back into her face. Determined, she kept bailing.

Three cans out, several gallons back in. The outboard rising out of the water, the engine spitting in the air. After several minutes, she yelled over to the caller. "You need to help."

He turned his face from her, dug under the stern and came up with another can. He started bailing on the other side, his can scraping against the deck.

A blinding flash of lightning split the darkness directly in front of them. Dawn's scream froze in her throat. Thunder roared overhead. It reverberated in her bones like a loud bass line. Less than five seconds had passed. They were in the eye of the storm. Desperate, she bailed faster. If this continued, these assholes wouldn't have a chance to kill her before they all ended up six feet under.

CHAPTER FIFTY-ONE

Dawn bailed. The wailing wind whipped the salty brine back into her face. Her hair was plastered to her head, water streamed down her neck, ran down her back. The lightning and thunder parried overhead like querulous lovers. The bow slammed down hard into a trough throwing her off balance. She teetered and landed hard on her left shoulder. The motor sputtered in the air, then quit.

Miguel turned the ignition repeatedly. Nothing. "Take the wheel," he yelled to the caller.

"And do what? There's no power."

"Try to keep her straight into the waves."

The man took over at the helm and Miguel skated over the deck to the stern, water sloshing up over his boots. The boat rolled and pitched, at the mercy of the oncoming waves. Grasping a rail, he leaned over the stern. The temptation to rush him was strong but Dawn resisted. There was no question in her mind that they'd quickly swamp without power. And where would she escape if the boat was out of commission?

Checking the gas can, he cursed loudly, his foul words carried off by the raging wind. He fell to one knee, dragged items out from under the stern. He returned to the helm. "We're out of gas. I'll call someone to come for us."

"I'll call," the caller said. "You take over here."

A rogue wave hit them broadside. Both Miguel and the caller went down. Dawn was thrown, her hip crushed into the gunwale. She cried out.

Miguel and the caller wrestled in a tangle of limbs. Water spilled in over the side. Miguel's eyes were wild. "I can't swim," he yelled. He arched his back, threw the other man off him, and scrambled toward the forward cubby. The caller followed him on all fours. Miguel pulled out a life jacket. The caller twisted it out of his hands. Miguel punched him in the face. Slack-jawed, the caller released it.

"I'll kill you for that," he yelled.

"I'd like to see you try." Kneeling, his balance precarious as the boat pitched side to side, Miguel shoved his arms into the life jacket and fumbled with the zipper.

The caller crawled into the cubby, only his ass visible. Dawn pushed herself up, terrified at the height of the wave rolling toward them. Ignoring the pain in her hip, she rushed for the wheel. Yanking it to the starboard, the small boat turned slightly into the path of the oncoming wall of water but it was too late.

It hit them broadside. She clenched the wheel in both hands, as water slammed into her torso and dragged her body to the side. More water spilled in over the port gunwale as they rocked dangerously close to capsizing. Spitting, she pulled herself back to the wheel and got her feet back on the deck as the boat pitched back, the muscles in her arm trembling with the strain.

In the cubby, the caller yelled, his words whipped away by the wind and the slosh of the water on the deck and the tremendous show of force above their heads as the lightning and thunder tangled the sky.

Miguel finally got his life jacket on and pushed himself to his feet. Dawn gave up the wheel. Her bailer bobbed in the water licking at her ankles. She lunged for it, filled it, emptied it, filled it, emptied it until she felt like a mechanical toy and her fingers cramped and the muscles in her arms ached and twitched.

She glanced back at Miguel. She knew she was missing another opportunity. But where would she go if the boat was out of commission?

The caller yelled at Miguel. "They're coming. We need to hang on until they get here." Dawn turned to see him emerge from the cubby, sliding his arms into a life jacket. He'd abandoned the tarp and a navy bandana covered his nose and mouth. His eyes were translucent. The coldest blue she'd ever seen. Like melting ice. They drifted over her, head to toe and back up again.

A shiver ran down her spine. Glued to the deck, she waited for his eyes to meet hers. He avoided her stare and turned to consult with Miguel at the wheel.

Dawn knew two things. If the eyes are a window to the soul, then his heart was as cold as his voice. And, if he planned to kill her, he wouldn't have bothered to hide his face.

She bailed faster.

CHAPTER FIFTY-TWO

Meg fought against the current, her arms growing weaker by the second. Her leg had stopped throbbing long ago and now was numb and dead weight. The constant slap of salt water in her face stung her eyes. She kept her mouth clamped shut, breathing through her nose between waves. Timothy faded in and out. His clothes had filled with air and he'd be easier to drag if it wasn't for the damn current fighting against her every stroke.

Lightning cracked to the north, lighting up the waves. She spotted the buoy and adjusted her direction. The waves and current kept pushing her off course and despite trying to compensate for it, it felt like she was losing more ground than she was gaining.

Thunder followed less than five seconds after. The storm was close. It raged around them. She'd lost track of how long they'd been in the water. She no longer had any hope that Dawn would return for them. The men in the speedboat had probably shot her, too.

The loss of her new friend was unbearable. But Dawn would not die in vain. Dawn had put everything on the line to save

Timothy - and later to save her - and Meg planned to stay alive if it was the last thing she did.

Against her chest, Timothy coughed and tried to push away. "Timothy, hold still," she said. He kept drifting in and out, and each time he came to he was disoriented, fighting and screaming. If she lived through this, she'd be bruised head to toe.

"Timothy, it's Meg," she said, for the hundredth time. "Stop fighting me."

In her arms, Timothy twisted, his hand squeezing her forearm. She cried out but refused to release him. "Stop."

He turned toward her, his arm wrapping around her waist, glued to her again. He kicked and punched with his other hand. In this position she couldn't hold him still. His feet started to sink, dragging her with him. She filled her lungs before they went under. He climbed up her body, his hands on her shoulders, pushing her farther down. Her legs gave out, she sank deeper as he clambered up her torso like a tree, his feet on her shoulders as he tried to claw his way back to the air.

Raising her arms, she pushed herself downward, farther under, and was free of him. Then she swam for the surface. She broke through two yards from him. His head swiveled on his neck, his eyes rolled in his head like a deranged puppet. He saw her and thrashed toward her. She had an idea.

Meg kicked backward, maintaining a distance between them, sometimes two yards, sometimes only one. Always just out of his reach. She hoped she was going in the right direction. Timothy coughed, his eyes flickered, but he kept lunging for her, reaching for something, anything, to hold onto.

Rain lashed down. Lightning sliced through the sky above. The thunder that followed deafened the howling wind. She kept her eyes on Timothy and kept pushing backwards. He was showing signs of exhaustion, starting to go under every few seconds. His eyes started to roll up into his head, the whites of his eyes eerie against the black waves rolling over them. Behind him, a large whitecap curled toward them.

She reached for him as he took one final lunge toward her. Her fingers groped through the water and found his wrist. She braced for the wave. It shoved them down, a dangerous dance of twirls and spins and out of control whirling beneath the surface. Down, deeper, down. The current dragged them and still she clung to Timothy's arm. He was unconscious again, his body limp.

Then just as suddenly, in the eddy of a large rock, the current released them and she kicked her way up, dragging him with her. When she broke through the surface this time, the red light flashed only a few yards away.

With the last of her strength, she clamped her arm around Timothy, his chin cupped in her palm, and kicked and pulled toward the safety of the buoy.

CHAPTER FIFTY-THREE

The storm raged relentlessly. Gusts of wind blasted across the boat. Dawn bailed. Out of the corner of her eye, she watched the drama unfolding between Miguel and the caller. She edged closer to catch what they were saying.

The caller loomed over Miguel, himself a giant of a man. "I understand you're nervous, you big pussy," he said. "Punching me was uncalled for."

Miguel lashed out, his forearm slamming into the other man's chest. "Stay the hell away from me, you arrogant ass. You're not in charge of me."

"Actually," he said, pointing his index finger in Miguel's face, "I am. So if you touch me again, I'll take you out."

"Take me out where? To the ballgame? I'd like to see you try." Miguel scoffed but his eyes never left the caller's face. "And no, you're not my boss. So back the hell off."

"For this job, I'm in charge. If you doubt that, you know who to talk to."

Miguel's eyes flashed then he blinked and turned his attention back to the wheel.

The caller took a small step back, leaving space between them. It was now or never. Dawn stepped forward into that small space. "I need a life jacket," she said.

"Life jacket?" Miguel laughed. "You're lucky you're still here. If it wasn't for—"

The caller coughed. Miguel's eyes narrowed, but he didn't finish his sentence. Dawn whipped her head around. "Life jacket," she said. The man's eyes stared into hers and sent a chill through her.

"There's only two. They'll be here soon. Keep bailing."

She tipped her chin up to maintain eye contact. "Who are you? I mean, after all our *chats* I'd like to know."

"Trust me, if I wanted you to know, you'd already know. Now get back to bailing or I'll tie you up and hang you overboard for shark bait."

She backed off several inches.

"That's a good idea," Miguel said. "We should tie her up before the others get her."

"We need her help bailing."

"For the transfer," Miguel said. "You don't know what this girl is capable of."

The caller scoffed. "So you keep saying. This itty bitty girl took you out last time? That's funny as hell. I mean, look at her, she's like a drowned rat." He looked down his nose at Dawn. "Barely big enough to hurt a flea."

His gaze swung back to Miguel. "A big, ugly flea apparently."

Miguel simmered and skewered him with a look of pure hatred. "You think you know so much. Just put the damn zip-tie on her hands."

Dawn backed away. The story of the Brer Rabbit from her childhood coming back to her. "No, not in this storm. We could capsize any minute. Come on," she protested. "If I go over, I'll die for sure."

The caller laughed. "Is this where we're all supposed to join hands and sing Kumbaya?"

"You don't have any sins to confess before you die?" she spat back.

"Hell, yeah. But nothing I wouldn't do again in a heartbeat." His cool eyes held hers.

Dawn stopped cold. She couldn't say the same. She had a shit ton of regrets.

"Besides," Miguel said, "maybe we *want* you dead."

She caught a look between the two men. "Then how come I'm not already dead?"

Miguel swung his arm and backhanded her across the face. She stumbled and landed on her ass, her nose bleeding. "If I had my way, you would be."

"Stop," the caller said to Miguel. "Freakin' big baby." But he dug in the console, grabbed a zip tie and crossed to where she was sprawled out.

"Hold your hands out in front of you." She pressed her wrists together and he placed the tie snuggly around her wrists. Grabbing her elbow, he helped her up and handed her the can. "Keep bailing."

It was awkward bailing with her hands secured in front of her. She planted her feet, legs apart, and hunched forward, dragging the can repeatedly along the floor between her feet and throwing the water out over the side.

The boat rocked steadily with the oncoming waves. Miguel kept working the wheel but the rudder did little in a squall like this.

"There," Miguel said. Through the rain, Dawn saw a white light approaching. Maybe that was south. Maybe not.

"There's no running lights," the caller said.

Miguel grunted. "Too dark to see them."

"The dark would make it easier to see them, moron." The caller shook his head. Above the kerchief, Dawn saw him roll his eyes as he turned away from Miguel and glared out into the darkness.

The light drew closer, dipping out of sight then bouncing back into view again. While the caller paced, Dawn started to strategize how she could use the chaos of moving to the new boat to her advantage.

CHAPTER FIFTY-FOUR

THE LIGHT BOBBED CLOSER. MIGUEL AND HIS NOT SO friendly pal grew increasingly restless. "I can't wait to get out of this damn rain," Miguel said.

Dawn peered into the downpour, straining for a first glimpse of the approaching boat. To get herself out of this, she needed to know how many were coming. Her plan had to be executed like clockwork. Her timing perfect. She was confident she could pull it off but she needed the missing pieces to the puzzle.

Finally she saw the boat behind the light. Wait. It wasn't a boat. It was a jet ski with a lone rider. Her plan disintegrated like so much sugar in sweet tea.

"What the hell," Miguel said. He stepped to the side and took a line as the jet ski came up alongside. "Jump on, we'll have to tie this off the back or it'll be smashed to bits."

"Hang on." The man in the yellow slicker stood and, balancing precariously, unhooked a gas can sitting behind him. He passed it up toward Miguel.

A wave hit them broadside and they rolled down into the surf. Miguel lurched forward, grabbed at the can. The man on the jet ski lost his grip, his hand dangerously close to the hull of the speedboat as it rolled into him. He yelled as the force of the waves pushed him into the ocean. Miguel fumbled the gas can, leaned farther out, and, huffing, brought it aboard.

Hindered by her bound hands, Dawn scrambled for the boat hook and passed it to the caller. He extended it and clawed at the empty waves where the man had gone under. Seconds ticked past. Lightning pierced the darkness.

"To the right," Dawn said. The man's head bobbed up in front of the jet ski. He clawed frantically at the machine. "Get him."

The caller leaned forward, extended the hook and the man reached for it just as the little craft rolled again. He was pushed under.

With the hook fully extended, the caller waited, holding the rod inches above the surface. The man burst through the surface and grasped at the pole.

Miguel shoved her aside and walked the jet ski toward the stern so the caller had room to pull the man in. Once he had him at the hull of the speedboat, the caller reached down and dragged the man, coughing and spewing, into the boat.

Plan B. She could clamber aboard the jet ski and take off while they were all distracted. She eyed the machine bouncing wildly off the stern. She'd never outrun them but she'd have a head start while they dealt with the gas. But they were armed and, despite not wanting to kill her, she was sure they'd have no qualms about shooting her when she tried to escape.

Miguel pushed her roughly out of the way. "Grab a funnel," he ordered, jutting his chin below the stern.

"Release me," she said, extending her arms.

"You'll manage," he growled.

She scrambled below the stern, found one and waited while he took off the gas cap. "Here," he said. After three tries, with the deck bucking like a bronco, she succeeded in placing the funnel in the can.

He braced the smaller gas can between his knees and got the spout to the funnel. Then he poured, cursing for the gas to go faster as the boat pitched and swayed around them. Gas splashed and spilled into the water at their feet.

When the last of the gas was emptied into their tank, he passed the can to Dawn. With both hands, she screwed the cover back on and kicked both it and the funnel beneath the stern.

The man who'd brought the gas sprawled against the opening to the cubby. The caller towered over him. "You were supposed to bring a boat. How do we get everybody back on that?" He waved toward the jet ski being tossed about by the waves.

"The other boat wouldn't start," he said. "This was the only option. It's why I brought gas."

The caller shook his head and toed the other man's foot. "Get ready, we're going back."

Miguel turned over the ignition. Nothing.

"Prime it," Dawn said.

Miguel slanted her a look, his heavy brows lowered. "Ya think? It's not working."

Dawn hurried to the stern, looked for the ball and pumped to get more gas into the lines. On the fifth try, the engine sputtered and came to life.

The jet ski rider stepped up beside her. He took one look at her then busied himself pulling in the machine. The waves tossed and rolled it. Tension threatened to snap the line. He grunted and pulled.

"Get that thing in here," said the caller. He stepped up in front of him, and helped him pull the small craft in. They walked it up along the side. "Hurry, you get on first."

Miguel was turning the boat into the worst of the waves. "You're going?"

"Not taking more chances on this floating tub." He nodded in Dawn's direction. "You bring her back. I'll send someone to the dock to wait for you."

"What about the sailboat?" Dawn yelled, as he straddled the seat and secured himself behind the driver. "Did you blow them up?"

He looked up at her, raised his brows. "Go," he said, clapping the other man on the shoulder.

"Tell me," she yelled.

His laugh carried back to her on the wind as the jet ski lumbered through the waves and disappeared through a curtain of rain.

CHAPTER FIFTY-FIVE

"You. Up front where I can see you." Miguel yelled at Dawn as he guided the boat to follow the same direction as the jet ski. Dawn edged up to stand behind the windshield. If she ducked, it kept some of the spray off her face. It was the smallest of blessings.

"You should untie me," she said. "Any more problems and you'll be on your own. I won't be able to help."

"Ha." He barked out a laugh. "I don't need your help."

"Who was that man?" she asked.

He raised a brow. "None of your business."

"He treated you like crap. I'm surprised you'd take that from him."

"You talk too much," Miguel said. He spun the wheel hard to the port as a wave bore down on them. They dipped into the trench and came up the other side, the hull of the small boat shuddering beneath their feet.

"Where is he?" Dawn said.

Miguel looked at her like she had a screw loose. He jutted his chin forward. "You just saw him leave."

"Not him. Dylan. Did he put you up to this?"

"Who's Dylan?"

"The guy who sent Erik."

"I hired Erik a few days ago to keep an eye on you. You saved me a bundle by killing him."

"You what?"

"You don't understand English? I hired him. Money talks."

"What about Dylan?"

He shrugged. "I don't know any Dylan." Another wall of water curled overhead and Miguel pushed the throttle forward and steered straight into it.

How much more of this could they take? She had no way of knowing how far they'd drifted, where they were exactly. Her thoughts went to Meg and Timothy.

"You shot my friends. Did you hit them?"

He grunted. "You're too attached to people. Geez, you're still whining about the old guy who died months ago."

"*Three* months," Dawn said, gritting her teeth. "Did you hit them?"

The corner of his lip twisted upward. "I always hit my target."

"You didn't hit her on my boat," Dawn said. "You took out my window instead."

"I thought she looked familiar," Miguel said. "Second time's the charm, I guess." He laughed, pleased with his joke.

Dawn's blood boiled. "You killed my friends," she said.

"And you killed mine." His large head swiveled and for a heartbeat he stared right at her. "My best friend."

"Probably your only friend," Dawn shot back.

Miguel's eyes darkened. "You—"

"Are you sure he's dead? I think I only grazed him. Did you even stop to see if he was dead or needed help?"

Miguel tried to backhand her. She stepped out of the way and he missed. Lightning crackled too close for comfort, lighting up the night around them.

"You'd be smart to shut up," Miguel said.

"Or what? You have orders not to kill me." She took a perverse pleasure in taunting him. If she was going to die today, she might as well die with a small bit of pleasure.

"There's worse things than dying," he said.

The crack of thunder overhead cut him off. The boat pitched wildly against the gale.

Dawn's heart beat faster. They were low, a wall of water surrounded them.

Miguel saw it, too, and gripped the wheel with both hands. His eyes darted wildly, searching for an opening. The waves and rain and wind buffeted and tossed the small boat. She felt like they were in a blender.

For a brief moment, she wondered how the mystery man was faring on the jet ski. Hopefully not well. She couldn't imagine them making it back through this.

Then the largest wave of the night crashed down on them and she was pushed off her feet and tumbling along the deck, taking in water.

CHAPTER FIFTY-SIX

THE WATER FORCED DAWN ALONG THE DECK LIKE A RAG DOLL and into the storage beneath the stern. Her back slammed into a gas can. Something sharp jabbed her shin. She clawed at the deck, hindered with her hands tied, but there was nothing to grab.

Miguel crashed into her, jamming her elbow into the post. As the water receded, he struggled to his feet. He large hand reached down and dragged her out onto the open deck. "Wake up," he said. "Time to die."

This time she knew she hadn't imagined it. He was quoting *Blade Runner.* "You can't kill me," she spat.

"Shut the hell up," he said. "We're both going to die today so I may as well get some satisfaction out of it."

"Big man, fighting a woman with her hands tied." Dawn was not ready to die at the hands of this moron.

He bared his teeth and shoved her toward the stern. "You deserve everything you get."

She twisted away from him. As he grabbed for her, she raised her hands over her head and brought them down fast, wrenching her hands outward. The zip tie snapped. Pivoting, she blocked Miguel's arm with her left forearm and landed a solid punch to his face with her right. His eyes registered shock when he saw she was loose.

"Yeah, game on, asshole," she said.

He jumped, throwing his full weight on her and bent her backwards over the stern. The engine was mere inches from the side of her head. As the boat rolled and the propeller lifted into the air, he reached for her shoulders and tried to force her face into the blades.

She arched her back and kneed him in the groin. His eyes narrowed and he cursed against the wind. He jabbed his elbow into her gut and the breath was knocked out of her. His hands found her neck. Déjà vu.

Water washed up over the stern. He held her beneath the waves until her lungs burned, his thumbs digging into her neck. She clawed blindly at his face, tore at his ears. He dragged her up out of the water and punched her in the face.

Her vision blurred. She spat out water and sucked in a breath before he plunged her back into the water, holding her down. She kicked her legs wildly. Her time to die? Hell, no.

His face hovered over her in the water, his grin a cruel caricature of evil. She started to drift, his face fading in and out.

She would end up at the bottom of the ocean, share the same watery death as Joe.

The stern of the boat lifted and a wave threw the bow nose down in a deep trough. Miguel reeled backward, his grip loosening. Her thumbs found his eyeballs. Wrapping her legs around his hips for leverage, she used the momentum of the wave to raise herself, digging her thumbs into his eyes.

He yelled in agony. The bow crashed down into the trough. The boat was immediately thrown back again, the stern dipping, and Dawn and Miguel slammed up against the stern.

No, not today. Using the momentum to her advantage, Dawn twisted so her back was against the wave. She pushed until Miguel was bent over the stern, his head underwater, then she sprang backwards, lifted his legs and pushed, sliding him farther into the ocean.

His big arms flailed, his fingers grasped at air. His hand trailed along the engine, blood whipped into the air as the propeller nicked him.

Grunting, she kept pushing. His butt, his legs. His feet. She stepped back as he slid free of the boat and his big brown boots dropped into the water.

CHAPTER FIFTY-SEVEN

DAWN CLAWED HER WAY BACK TO THE WHEEL, DRAGGING herself back with the rails along the gunwale. The water in the boat was mid-way up her shins. Another wave hit her broadside, and the boat listed to the port, water rushing in.

She was going to lose the boat. It would swamp. She got her hands on the wheel and wrenched it toward the oncoming wave. The bow bucked in protest. The engine sputtered as it lifted out of the water again. She kept turning, the wave hovering over her. For a split second, all she saw above was suspended water, it dripped down on her, a teaser of what was to come.

The wave crashed into the boat and she held steady to the wheel, operating on gut instinct, holding the bow as much in a straight line as was possible. Her fingers ached on the wheel. Her throat burned. She bit the inside of her cheek to ground herself, then yelled into the wind. "It's not my time to die."

Water sloshed around her legs, the boat lurched to the starboard, and then righted. Her feet remained solidly on the deck. Her hands gripped the wheel, knuckles white. Terrified, she scanned the wall of water surrounding her and chose a path, turning the wheel into the next oncoming wave.

Lightning flared overhead and she turned, peering into the churning waters off the stern. For a second, she thought she saw a flash of orange, Miguel's life jacket bobbing on the waves. She wanted to be sure he was dead.

It didn't matter. The only path to her own salvation lay ahead.

CHAPTER FIFTY-EIGHT

Exhausted beyond anything she'd ever experienced, Meg clung to a cleat on the navigation buoy, her fingers cramped, her arms aching. Her lids were heavy. She drifted into sleep and snapped awake when her chin hit the water.

Timothy's head rested on the other side of the buoy, each flash of the blinking red light illuminated his pale skin. It helped reassure her that he was still breathing. He hadn't been conscious in a long time.

When they reached the buoy, she'd discovered the gunshot in his upper arm. No wonder he'd fought her so hard each time she'd grabbed him. She'd used the bungee to bind his wrists together around the buoy, keeping his head above the surface. The buoy danced and weaved on the turbulent seas and Timothy's cheeks would be bruised and battered. But he'd be alive.

The storm ravaged them. Waves slammed into them, walls of water washed over them. There was so much salt water in her belly she felt nauseous.

It had been hours. Or minutes. She'd lost track of time. Exhaustion threatened to overcome her. Pain thrummed in so many areas of her body she could no longer focus.

It felt like the storm was backing off. But that could be wishful thinking. Lightning flickered overhead, bathing everything around her in an eerie light. She could swear she saw farther into the gloom this time, that the rain was slowing down. Were her eyes playing tricks on her?

If nothing else, she'd had a front row seat to the light show of the century. Thunder crashed overhead and set her teeth to chattering.

She was still breathing.

The storm had beat them down but it hadn't beaten her.

Not yet.

CHAPTER FIFTY-NINE

Dawn couldn't get her bearings. She steered the boat north, following the needle that bobbled on the compass. She had no way of knowing how far they'd drifted, whether the island was behind her or lay somewhere ahead.

She was determined to find her way back to the channel, back to the spot where she'd lost Meg and Timothy.

Each time lightning lit the sky she searched for a landmark. A horizon. A shoreline. Still nothing.

The storm was receding, the ride over the waves not as jarring. She no longer feared for her life with each roll. Her hands rode easily on the wheel, no longer like holding the reins on an unruly horse.

A ton of water sloshed around her legs. There wasn't a damn thing she could do about it. She focused on the waves in front of her and maintained a heading as close to north as she could manage.

Rain continued to fall but visibility was better and she no longer felt like she was in a wind tunnel. Occasionally, she switched on the spotlight but never for long. It took too long to recover her night vision.

She could swear the sky overhead was not crowding in as low as before. Did she really see a band of light to the east?

The long night was coming to an end.

She was still here.

And she was going to find her friends.

CHAPTER SIXTY

THE BUOY RODE THE WAVES, THE MOTION ALMOST GENTLE. The waters were growing calmer. Meg watched the light flash on. Off. On. Off. Lids heavy, she counted the light and struggled to stay awake.

She could make out the point to the south now, and the sharp jagged rocks. Getting them ashore no longer seemed like an option. Her strength was gone, her limbs felt boneless.

The island to the north was farther away. It had a better shoreline. At least what she could see of it from this distance. But she knew she'd never make it. Their best chance was hanging onto this light. Eventually a boat would come along. She only hoped they'd last until it did.

Timothy grumbled in his sleep, his cheek glued to the wet red metal. A wave lapped at his neck.

Overhead a pair of vultures soared on the updrafts.

Meg peered into the east. Her heart lifted. A thin band of light graced the haze of the horizon. Soon it would be day.

To the west, she saw another navigation buoy dancing over the waves. No, it was moving. A boat. She yelled.

Desperate, she hauled herself up onto the buoy, grabbing

Timothy's forearms to drag herself up. He woke and yelped in pain.

Meg tried to get herself out of the water, to make herself more visible. She yelled until she was hoarse.

The green light chugged farther northward, her frustration finally released and tears rolled down her cheek, dashing away the desperation of the night.

She slipped back into the water. It was only a matter of time now until another boat came for them. With the approaching dawn, came the slightest glimmer of hope.

"Where are we?" Timothy said. "What the hell is going on?"

"We're still above the surface," Meg said. "Stay calm. They'll come for us."

"Who?"

"Someone," Meg said, head lolling to the side. "Someone will come for us. Keep talking, Timothy, I need you to keep me awake."

"Who are you?" he asked. "Untie me!" He kicked in the water but she'd tied him securely.

Meg tried to ignore his yelling and fixed her eye on the rocky point. She watched the tips of the rocks dip in and out of the waves.

Were the rocks moving? Was she so tired she was hallucinating now?

Then she realized she wasn't looking at rocks. She started to hyperventilate and her throat closed in panic.

She was looking at fins.

The sharks were circling.

CHAPTER SIXTY-ONE

DAWN PUSHED THE BOAT AS FAST AS SHE DARED. THE STORM was backing off. Less lightning. Less thunder. The murky but promising weak glow of twilight gave her hope.

To the east, she spotted shoreline. She continued north, keeping the shoreline on her right.

To the west loomed land. Through the rain she spied a sandy beach, a long, low home with a red roof, a pier with a large Chris Craft. She remembered this property from the trip down. She was too far north. She turned the boat and headed due south, against the wind.

The water was not as choppy as before, but it was still rough. The boat skimmed roughly over the waves, jarring what was left of her nerves.

On her left she ran out of shoreline and spotted the navigation light that would guide boaters through the channel. It blinked as the last of the night scurried away from the approaching day.

Keeping the light in her sights, Dawn pushed the boat faster. The engine whined. There. Some movement on the buoy.

She cursed, wished for binoculars. She pushed faster, the engine working hard as she plowed through the waves.

There was definitely movement on the buoy. The base was thicker than it should be near the water. She made out a darker shape against the red metal. She cut the power back as she cruised into the channel, hugging the shore of the northern island.

Yes. There was someone on the buoy. She gasped. There were two figures. Her friends had made it through the night. She screamed into the wind and waved back at Meg.

At the same time she spotted them, she saw the vultures overhead. When her eyes dropped back to the surface, she saw the fins circling the buoy behind Meg and Timothy.

Sharks. Had she come this far only to lose them now?

She accelerated, bringing the power up as much as she dared in the rocky channel. She pushed the boat past the buoy, past Meg screaming at her, and turned the boat so it was between her friends and the sharks. She threw Meg a line. While Meg struggled to hold her fast, she grappled with the boat hook that was stuck on something under the stern. Finally it came free and she glanced over the port side. The sharks were keeping their distance. For now.

"Tie me off and I'll get you on board."

Meg's hands trembled as she worked to thread the line through the cleat. The skin on her hands was puckered and looked like molded oranges. "Get Timothy first," Meg said. "I need to untie him."

"Timothy." Dawn called down to him. "He's barely awake."

"I know," Meg said. "Where are the sharks?"

Dawn glanced to the side. "Still there." Meg was unwinding the bungee cord that secured Timothy's arms to the buoy. "Wait. Keep one end of that around his wrist and then pass it to me."

Meg released one of Timothy's arms, then wrapped the

bungee tighter around his wrist. He was already sliding off the buoy. "I can't hold him," she said.

"Pass me the cord." Dawn leaned over the side, extending her arm. The boat rocked under her, she stretched her fingers as Meg tried to get it to her. She grabbed it and shimmied back until her feet were solidly on deck again, her legs braced against the gunwale. "Can you help push him?"

"I don't have much strength left," Meg said. "I'll try."

"You'll need to get in the water."

Meg's eyes darted wildly into the open water. "Where are the sharks?"

Dawn got her hand around Timothy's wrist and started to drag him over the side. "Still circling but they're not close. I need your help, Meg."

"God help me," Meg said, under her breath. Dawn barely heard her. As Meg moved to the other side of the buoy, Dawn dragged Timothy in by one arm, until she could grasp him under his armpit. Moments later she had his torso over the boat.

"Get out of the water," Dawn said to Meg.

"Are they coming?" Her voice was shrill. She clawed at the navigation buoy but the slick metal gave her no purchase.

"No, you're okay." She dumped Timothy into the water at her feet and turned her full attention to Meg. Grabbing the hook, she extended it. "Come on, climb up," she said. "I've got you."

Hand over hand, Meg pulled herself to the boat, Dawn sliding the hook back at the same time.

Dawn grabbed Meg's wrist and pulled her in over the side while Meg kicked. They landed together in a jumble of legs and arms.

CHAPTER SIXTY-TWO

With Meg and Timothy finally safe, Dawn turned her attention to the next task. She maintained a heading due north, up the eastern coast of the island, heading back to the cove where they'd seen the sailboat.

"Do you know if they blew it up?" Meg knelt on the deck, administering to Timothy. She'd propped his head up on a flutter board and kept giving him small sips of fresh water. He was in rough shape. Beaten, exhausted, bloody and bruised. One of the bullets had grazed his upper arm. The night hanging off the buoy with most of his body in the water hadn't helped his condition.

"He wouldn't say. And Miguel..." She shrugged. "Let's just say we didn't get to it. You know anything they'd say would be a total lie anyway."

"Maybe we would have heard the explosion if they blew it up?" Meg looked up at Dawn. Meg's face was pale, her lips almost blue. Water dripped out of her hair and down over her shoulders. At this moment, she looked weak. But Dawn was coming to appreciate that, despite appearances, Meg was tough as steel.

"In that storm? No. All we can do is get there and hope for the best."

Timothy drifted back to sleep and Meg pushed herself off the floor, shaking out her legs.

"How's the leg?"

"Messed up," she said. She turned, grab one of the metal containers and started bailing water out. She paused and turned back to Dawn. "We should call the Coast Guard."

"Sure. Where's your phone?"

Meg crooked her head to the right. "Gone to the land of dead phones. Yours?"

"Same."

"No radio on board?"

Dawn held up the handset. A severed wire dangled off the end. "Besides, we're not going to come off smelling like roses. It was self-defense but it'll come down to our word against theirs. If they even find them."

"Erik is dead." It wasn't a question. Meg crossed her arms. Dawn kept her eye on the horizon. "I heard what he said. I don't understand how Miguel got to him. I mean, how twisted is that?" She sucked in a breath and shook her head. "He saw what those men are capable of."

"Money," Dawn said. She could have shot him in the leg. Taken him out of commission. But he'd pushed her too far and she'd lost her temper. "When I first realized he was working with them, I thought he had a link to Dylan."

"Wait. Who's Dylan?"

"The guy responsible for Joe's death."

"Related to the court case you're involved in?"

Dawn hadn't talked a lot about that with Meg and she didn't plan to now. "Yes, but the court case involves two of Dylan's guys. They haven't found Dylan yet."

"So maybe linking Erik to Dylan was premature?"

"It was his Irish accent that made me suspicious," Dawn said. "Dylan was also Irish. Also from Boston."

Meg tapped her chin with her finger. "Is it possible you're a little paranoid about that whole thing?"

Dawn laughed. "Considering what I've been through recently, I would say I'm not paranoid enough. But Miguel confirmed that he hired Erik and said he'd never heard of Dylan. Anyway, life hasn't exactly been shouting at me that it's safe to trust people lately."

"Maybe not," Meg said. "Or before that either, I'm guessing."

Dawn slanted her a look. "Maybe you could check on Timothy again."

———

Twenty minutes later, Dawn spotted the mouth of the cove. "We're here," she said.

Meg ditched the container and came to stand beside her. Dawn was grateful for the company. Just as she'd been grateful for the quiet over the past twenty minutes. She and Meg worked well together. It had been a hell of a way to have to find that out.

She navigated into the cove. Not until she spotted the sailboat at the far end, did she realize she'd been holding her breath. She exhaled noisily.

"I know, right?" Meg shook her head. "I kept thinking of this couple all night long. I guess Bill did what they needed him to do and they let them live. Do you think..."

"What? That if we'd paid for Timothy they would have let him go? No." Dawn's no was clipped.

"You sound pretty sure."

Dawn turned and looked down at Timothy. "Yeah, I'm sure. Anyway, they had the money, remember? I did pay."

She powered back. It was early. The sun still sitting low on the horizon. The last of the storm had been whisked away, the surface of the small cove calm and flat.

"I'm surprised this boat is still at anchor. Lucky they were so sheltered overnight." And for the first time, she thought about her own boat. About the Papa Joe. What kind of mess might she go back to there? She hoped the anchor had held.

"I don't see anyone."

"Me either." The boat looked the same as it had the day before. Still closed up, the curtains drawn, but as she idled up close to the stern she saw that this time there was a dingy with a small outboard and the door had been closed from inside. She motioned to Meg. "There's someone here and the padlock is gone."

"Do you think they're still tied up in there? Want me to go aboard and check?"

"Hello," Dawn called out. "Anyone here?" She searched the console for a horn, but there was nothing. She called out again, louder, as she idled past the stern and turned to go around again. A curtain in the porthole near the bow rippled. "There's someone there," she said, lowering her voice. "We'll give them a few minutes, and if nobody comes out, you'll have to go aboard." She remembered the video and the size of the bomb strapped to the man's chest. "Or I will."

As they floated near the stern again, she indicated to Meg to take the wheel. "I'll go," she said. "At this point, I'm in better shape than you."

"If there's a dingy here, somebody else might be there," Meg said. "It's too dangerous."

Dawn reached up and grabbed onto a rail at the back. "Stay here," she said. "I'll just have a quick look."

Her pulse raced. Meg was right. Somebody else had to be onboard. She drew her weapon.

She knew nothing about bombs. If they were still in there,

what could she do? It would be too risky to move them. Hopefully they had a working radio and she could call for help.

She hoisted herself up. As her foot hit the deck, the hatch opened and a large figure filled the doorway. Her mouth dropped open and she stared up into the face of Captain Wayne Cutter.

CHAPTER SIXTY-THREE

"Dawn." Cutter stepped out onto the deck and threw his hands up in front of his chest. Dawn was still armed. "What the hell?"

What the hell indeed? What was Cutter doing out here? She lowered her weapon.

"Wayne. Did you already get the call?" Her head swiveled around the small cove. "Where's your vessel?"

"The Serenity Jane *is* my vessel." His brow creased as he gave her an appraising look. She knew she looked like a drowned rat. The gash on her leg was puffy and crusted with dried blood. "Sit," he said, taking her elbow and guiding her onto the gunwale.

Wayne took in Meg's face, a labyrinth scratches and bruises. A large goose egg adorned a deep cut on her forehead.

"Cherie, get up here!" He yelled over his shoulder. "Bring the first aid kit."

Finally, his gaze fell on Timothy, prone and bloody in the bottom of the boat.

"What the hell is going on here?" he said, frowning. "Thank God you found me."

Dawn choked and glanced down to Meg for help. Meg shrugged, as confused as she was. "We didn't find you. We—"

"You obviously need help. Have your friend throw me a line." Wayne took the line Meg passed up and brought them alongside. He tied it off to a cleat then handed a line down to Meg so she could secure the stern.

"Wayne? Are you okay?" A curvy woman in a pink slip of a nightie stepped out on deck. "Oooh," she said, her eyes quickly running over Dawn and Meg and fixing on Timothy. Her heavily-shadowed eyes widened. "What's going on here?" She held the first aid kit out to Wayne.

"Grab some warm water and clean towels. And put some coffee on."

Cherie backed away through the hatch. Seconds later, the sound of running water and the pump working drifted up from below.

Wayne extended his hand to Meg and helped her on deck. "What happened to your leg?"

Dawn ignored his question, her eyes darting to Meg. "Wayne, what are you doing here? We were told there's a couple being held hostage on this boat. Do you have explosives on board?"

"What?" His brow furrowed. "You need to start at the beginning. And why haven't you called the Coast Guard?"

"No phones," Meg said.

"Your boat doesn't have a radio?"

"No, and it's not our boat," Dawn said. "Do you have a bomb on board or not?"

"Clearly not. This is becoming more convoluted by the second. First things first. What kind of injuries does your friend have?" He clambered over the side and down into the speedboat.

"Not sure exactly. He was badly beaten and has a gunshot

wound in the upper arm," Dawn said. "He's been mostly uncon-scious since we rescued him from the kidnappers."

"Kidnappers?" Wayne knelt over Timothy and checked the pulse in his neck. "Are his injuries life-threatening?"

"He needs medical but he made it through the night and he's no longer losing blood," Dawn said. "He could have internal injuries."

Wayne nodded, one quick tilt of his chin. "Start at the begin-ning. Cliff notes. I only want to know what's essential so I can get you some help." He climbed back on board the Serenity Jane.

Dawn paused a beat. As much as she wanted justice for Timothy, she was responsible for Erik's death and possibly both Jose's and Miguel's. She hoped the courts would accept her version of events and believe it was self-defense.

Dawn rushed through the story, occasionally glancing to Meg to see if she'd left anything out.

"Wait," he said. "They showed you a video of a couple tied up with explosives on this boat?"

"Yes. It looked very real. It also showed the transom with the name Serenity Jane."

He waved his hand toward the cabin. "You've been had," he said.

"But were you here last night? Maybe while you were away."

"We've been out here a couple of days," he said.

"But you gave me a drive to the bank yesterday."

"When I saw you yesterday, I was killing time in town while Cherie had an appointment, but we were back just after sunset." He paused. "I don't know why they'd choose this boat to give you such a scare."

"I know why," she said. "It's because of what happened in this cove last time I was here."

"The whole thing that Birch helped you out with?"

She nodded. "They must have shot the video somewhere

else and just happened to find this sailboat in this cove at the precise time they needed it."

Wayne's eyes cut to Meg. "You kept this guy on the buoy all night, during that storm? I'm impressed."

Dawn interrupted before Meg could respond. "Wayne, this is the woman Captain Birch recommended for CG training."

He appraised her again and nodded slowly. "I agree with Birch. You'd be a great candidate."

"That means a lot, sir," Meg said.

Wayne turned to Dawn and put his hand over hers. "You two have had a hell of a night." He stood up. "I'll put a rescue call in."

"What about the kidnappers?"

"I'll ask them to send someone out there to check things out. It's a long shot though, I'm sure they're long gone by now."

"The bodies will still be there," Dawn said.

"One thing at a time. I'll make the call and then we can get you two patched up while we wait."

Dawn stood. "I can't wait. I'm going back to the Papa Joe now."

"You're kidding, right? There could be someone waiting for you. It's not safe."

"I need to get back to Joe's boat."

Cherie came up with a large bowl of steaming water and a pile of towels. Wayne nodded at her. "Thanks. Can you also grab a blanket for him?" He tilted his head toward Timothy.

Wayne turned away and Cherie held out the towels to Dawn and Meg. "You're both so pale," she said. "Please stay with us."

"No, but thank you" Dawn shook her head and climbed down into the speedboat. She reached up to help Meg down.

"I'll grab a blanket for your friend," Cherie said. Then she called out, "Wayne."

Wayne came back. "You're not going to wait? The medics are on their way."

"Can you ask them to intercept us?"

"I can, but it's dangerous for you to go back to the Papa Joe alone."

"I'm going," Dawn said. She tried to ignore Wayne's glare but the strong sense of foreboding wouldn't leave her. There was no way she could sit on the Serenity Jane waiting to be rescued. "Can you untie us?"

Wayne sighed. "Fine, I'll have them intercept you but it won't be before you get to your boat." He turned to Cherie. "Do you have that coffee ready?"

Timothy hadn't shifted an inch while they'd been talking. Cutter jerked his head toward him. "You'll be heading toward them so it will save some time and get your friend to the medics faster. That's the only reason I'm agreeing to this insanity, Dawn."

Cherie got his attention and he took the blanket she passed up and tossed it down to Meg. Meg spread it carefully over Timothy.

Wayne glared down at Dawn. "You're leaving against my strong recommendation that you wait."

Dawn had no intention of changing her mind. "I hear you, but we're going."

"I'll send Cherie's phone with you. I'm in her contacts. If you get to your boat and sense any trouble, I want you to call me. Can you do *that* at least?"

"I appreciate that," Dawn said.

Cherie came back on deck with several bottles of water and a bag filled with snacks and passed it to Dawn. "Hang on, I also have a thermos of coffee for you."

"Grab your phone, too, Cherie," Wayne said. She opened her mouth, decided against saying anything, and disappeared inside. When she returned, she passed a thermos and cups to Dawn, then fished her phone out of her pocket and passed it to Wayne.

"Passcode?"

"1-2-3-4."

"Seriously?" He passed the phone to Dawn. "I'm sure you'll remember that."

"Thanks, Wayne." Dawn turned the ignition.

"Please be careful," Cherie said.

Dawn appreciated the sentiment but exhaled a breath as she pulled away. Help was on the way and the worst was behind them.

CHAPTER SIXTY-FOUR

"WHAT'S OUR RUNNING TIME?" MEG SAID. SHE STOOD BESIDE Dawn, carefully pouring steaming coffee into the mugs Cherie had provided. Dawn's mouth watered as she watched.

"Not much longer," Dawn said. A slight breeze had chased away the last of the storm clouds. Wisps of cotton candy skittered across the blue sky above. The day promised to be hot, sunny, and clear. Dawn couldn't wait to get out of it and lay her head on her pillow in her snug little bunk.

Timothy stirred and Meg gave him water and one of the granola bars. He grumbled about the taste of blood in his mouth and slipped under again.

Meg rose and took a sip of her coffee. "What do you make of that video with the couple and the bomb, all on Cutter's boat? Why go to so much trouble?"

"Leverage," Dawn said. She thought back to the image of the couple, the terror in their eyes. "It was effective. I'm just glad there wasn't actually a bomb to defuse."

"You and me both. But what about Bill? Was it all an act?"

"I don't know," Dawn said. "If it was, he was a hell of an

actor. I guess it would explain why Erik was so insistent we take him hostage."

"How so?"

"Having Bill cooperate with us, or help us, would have made the whole plan go sideways. I think Erik steered things so they could go off together, ahead of us."

"I suppose we'll never know for sure." Meg rolled her mug between her hands and scanned the horizon. "Do you think it will take the CG long?"

"You would know response times better than me, wouldn't you?"

Meg cracked a smile. "I was a little intimidated by Captain Cutter."

Dawn shrugged. "He's a good guy. You impressed him."

Meg stepped across the cabin, put her weight down on her bad leg and flinched. "This trip will be like college all over again. Did you ever do that after a drunken party? Compare bruises the next day?"

"Yeah. Unfortunately, I was doing that long past college." Dawn stared out over the waves. Hard to believe they could coast along so peacefully after the storm that ravaged them only hours before.

"Hey, Dawn, there's something I've been wanting to ask you."

"Hold that thought," Dawn said. She'd had people broach this question so many times she could see it coming and she didn't want to get into it right now. "Can you put some bumpers down? We'll be there in five minutes."

"What if there's someone waiting for us?" Meg said.

"If we see somebody on board, we'll turn back and call Wayne."

Dawn slowed the speedboat as they entered the small cove. By her calculations, the Papa Joe had dragged anchor during the storm. Probably by fifty yards or so. No harm had come from that and she rested on the flat surface of the crystal water, sunlight reflecting off the forward window.

"See, there's no dingy. All quiet."

As Dawn cruised up past the boat, she noticed the wheelhouse door open. She clenched her teeth. "I locked that door," she said.

"Yeah, you did. Everything was locked up when we left."

Dawn ran the speedboat up along the port side. Meg secured a line to a cleat and crawled up on deck to toss another line down to Dawn. Dawn tied it off and hauled herself up onto her boat.

She hurried to the wheelhouse and stood frozen in the center of the cabin surveying the wreckage, a fist gripping her heart.

Meg entered and gasped. "What the hell?"

Every chart, everything item on the chart table had been swiped to the floor. The wheelhouse bench stood open, empty, all items stored beneath thrown in a pile. The drawers of the chart table stood on their sides, some broken, kicked apart, others upside down. Dawn's pulse raced.

"Oh, hell, Dawn." Meg's voice came from the galley. Dawn ignored her and raced down the steps to the forward cabin. The bedding and mattresses were strewn on the floor. The hinged wooden cover stood open. A piece of the combination lock glinted on the starboard bunk. She knew before she reached it that the locker would be empty.

Scrambling over the mattresses, she peered into the bottom of the metal box. An icy chill ran through her. She hugged her stomach and bent low over the empty space.

While she'd been fighting for her life in the middle of the storm, forty thousand dollars had walked off her boat.

CHAPTER SIXTY-FIVE

DAWN ROCKED IN PLACE, BARELY AWARE OF THE HEAT IN THE small cabin. Forty thousand dollars. Yesterday she'd been flush, today she was busted.

"You okay?" Meg yelled down the stairs.

"Coming," Dawn said. She picked her way back toward the wheelhouse, her eye landing on the board beneath the starboard porthole where the automatic rifle was still secreted. It remained untouched, still in place. At least they hadn't found that.

Meg stood in the middle of the wheelhouse and gestured at the mess at her feet. "You want me to pick up this stuff?"

"We need to get underway. The CG will be here soon and Timothy needs medical attention." She stepped to the console. The radio was gone, jagged wires hung from the mount, the handset jiggling on the end of the cable like a cat's plaything.

"Anything missing?" Meg said.

"I had some cash down below." She glanced back at the clock to check the time. They'd smashed that, too. Joe had loved that clock.

"You mean, you had more on board than the ten grand you brought for the kidnappers?"

"Yeah." *Easy come, easy go right?* She struggled to rationalize the loss. Yesterday morning she had nothing. Twenty-four hours later - same. Her gut clenched. She could have done so much with that money.

"Oh." Meg's eyes darted to the side, embarrassed by the surprise in her statement. "I don't mean to be ... indelicate but I figured the ten grand would have wiped you out."

"Most days you'd be right about that," Dawn said. "But I had to pull all the money out and didn't have time to get back to my bank." She shook her head. She still felt like she was going to throw up. "It's a long story. Let's get out of here." The only way she could cope was to stay busy.

Meg pursed her lips. "Okay. You want to check the galley before we go?"

"Can I assume it's a mess?"

"Trashed," Meg confirmed. "What about Timothy? We'll have to wake him to get him on board."

"Let's get that done," Dawn said. "Then we need to get the hell out of here."

CHAPTER SIXTY-SIX

TWENTY MINUTES UNDER WAY, MEG POINTED TO A SPOT ON the horizon. "Coast Guard." Meg had dug through the mess on the cabin floor earlier and found the binoculars. She handed them to Dawn.

"Good. We'll maintain this heading and they'll intercept us."

"Yeah, good thing we ran into Captain Cutter. I mean, no phones, no radios. What would we have done without him?"

Dawn nodded. Indeed. The man certainly had a knack for showing up when she needed him most.

Meg turned back to the items on the floor. "Want me to stow this stuff away? Or do you want to go through it first, see what might be missing?"

"Just leave it," Dawn said.

"Can't. Timothy's sleeping. I'm antsy." She picked up one of the drawers still intact and slid it into the chart table.

"Go ahead and stow it. I'll do inventory later."

"What about insurance? Will you put a claim in? You think the adjuster will want to see things as they are?"

Dawn shook her head. "There's nothing much of value on board." *Anymore.*

Meg worked, straightening out charts, replacing the drawers, putting the rest of the items into the storage area beneath the bench. By the time the CG reached them, the wheelhouse looked almost back to normal with the exception of the splintered drawers piled on top of the chart table.

"Bumpers?" Dawn asked.

"Still down," Meg said. "I forgot to bring them up. I'll get a line ready."

Dawn powered back as the CG vessel came up alongside. Once they were tied up, the Captain greeted her and two Coasties and a medic jumped onboard at the stern.

Dawn invited the Captain aboard. He stepped into the wheelhouse and his gaze fell on the empty radio mount. "You have no communications?"

"Someone broke into my boat overnight," Dawn said.

"Cutter didn't mention that."

"He didn't know. I discovered it when I returned."

The Captain stepped to the entrance to the galley. "Do you mind?"

"Go ahead." She followed him down and surveyed the mess. Every cupboard had been emptied. Plates and utensils lay atop jumbled piles of canned goods and partially broken open boxes of dry goods.

He whistled. "This'll take some cleaning up," he said. That was an understatement. Dawn ran her hand over her forehead, unable to continue ignoring her building tension headache. "You know who did this?"

"Pretty good idea," she said, looking around.

He stepped through the mess and out onto the back deck. "Look, I'm going to get your friend to the hospital. I want you to head straight back to the marina and then you and the other woman get to the hospital yourselves. Got it?"

"That's the plan," she said.

"You have a phone on board? Any communications at all?"

"Wayne, I mean Captain Cutter, lent me a cell."

"Good," he said. "I'm going to call out another boat to escort you back to the marina."

"That's not necessary," she said.

He raised a brow. "Head straight for the marina. They'll intercept you and follow you in." He tipped his hat and returned to his boat.

Relief eased the tension in her head. Just a touch. Necessary or not, she was grateful she wouldn't have to be looking over her shoulder all the way back in.

She'd had enough.

CHAPTER SIXTY-SEVEN

"Ma'am, ten more minutes until visiting hours are over." The nurse adjusted the IV line inserted into Timothy's wrist and whisked away, her rubbery soles silent on the glossy sterile floor.

Ma'am again.

Dawn closed her book and shoved it in a small backpack. On the bedside table, she inventoried the items she'd brought in for him. Toiletries, a notebook and pen, two paperback detective novels. A cheap phone she'd picked up at 7-11 and loaded with her new number and enough of a balance to make a few calls.

She'd picked up a change of clothes and folded it neatly into the locker and jammed his dirty clothes into a plastic bag to take to the laundry.

She didn't know what else she could do for him. The machine behind his head beeped steadily. She stood and headed for the door.

"Dawn." His voice was quiet, hoarse. She hurried back to his bedside. He reached out his hand and she grasped his fingers. "Where the hell am I?"

"Hospital."

"I feel like crap." He coughed.

A large bandage covered his nose. Both eyes were blackened. A lattice of stitches laced up one cheek, the other was purple and swollen. His arm was bandaged, his chest wrapped. "Honestly, you don't look much better." She tried to smile, but, mortified, burst into tears instead.

He squeezed her fingers. "Freak, Dawn, you're scaring me now."

Tears slid down her cheek. "You've been out for over a day. I was worried."

"What did the doctors say?"

"Timothy, I'm so sorry. I'm—"

"I thought I was going to die," he said.

Dawn's lip trembled and the tears flowed more freely. He squeezed her hand. "What did the doctors say?" he asked again.

She swiped the moisture from her cheeks and swallowed, collecting herself. "You're going to be fine. You have some internal injuries but you're on the mend." She gestured to the table near his head. "I brought you some things."

"How long will I be here?" He struggled to sit up.

"No," she said, planting a hand on his chest. "You need rest. They're not sure. Maybe a few days more. Do you need anything from home?"

The door swept open and the nurse poked her head in. "Visiting hours are over."

"He just woke up," Dawn said. "Can't I—"

"No," she said, rushing to his bedside. She pressed the call button. "Mr. Talbert, how are we feeling?"

"I brought you a phone," Dawn said. "My number is in it."

"You can come back tomorrow," the nurse said, waving her away. The door opened again and a young intern came in, followed by another nurse.

"Okay," Dawn said, backing to the door. The intern and two nurses hovered over Timothy. Her view of him was blocked. She almost missed the words he spoke as she went through the doorway.

"Thank you, Dawn."

CHAPTER SIXTY-EIGHT

DAWN PLACED THE LAST OF THE DRAWERS IN THE CHART table and stood back to admire her handiwork. Not bad. The facing on the third one down was slightly crooked but she'd never claimed to be a cabinet maker. It would do.

After she stowed the tools back in the large tool chest she'd borrowed from Timothy's boat, she swept up the remaining splinters and sawdust.

She took a look around. The wheelhouse was back to normal. Better than normal. Thomas Duncan, Joe's lawyer who had finalized her inheritance of the boat, had called claiming to find some funds previously unaccounted for. With some of the money he'd sent over, she'd purchased and installed a new radio.

The only thing missing was the clock. She'd taken it in for repair. They'd promised it back for later in the week. She'd asked them to engrave Joe's name and date of death on the back. It was sentimental, but hell. The tightness she'd been living with was loosening its grip on her. She felt a softening, like some of her rough edges were being buffed smooth.

"Permission to come aboard." Meg's voice called up to her from the dock. Dawn hadn't known she was coming. As she stepped across the cabin to greet her, she realized she liked that. A friend dropping by unannounced. What would surely have been an annoyance in the recent past brought a smile to her face.

"Hey," she said, popping her head out the door. "Great to see you."

"You, too." Meg took the hand Dawn extended, stepped up on board and followed Dawn into the wheelhouse. "Wow, things are looking good here."

Dawn smiled. "All back to normal."

"Is that a new radio?" Meg stepped over to the console. "Shiny."

Dawn laughed. "Yep. You sure have a way with words."

Meg laughed and held up the handset. "It's even attached. High-tech."

Dawn laughed again. Meg hugged her spontaneously. Dawn didn't pull away.

"I was in to see Timothy, so I thought I'd swing by," Meg said. "You busy?" She nodded toward the tool chest.

"Just finishing up. Got time for some iced tea?"

"Sounds good."

Dawn grabbed a pitcher and a couple of glasses from the galley and joined Meg at the little bistro table she'd put back up on the stern. Was it only a handful of days since they'd had lunch there?

Meg poured while Dawn adjusted the colorful umbrella to shield them from the mid-day sun.

When she was done she sat and reached for the glass in front of her. "Wayne called me. Said the resort is a dead end. His guys didn't find anything."

"Not even Erik or Jose? How is that possible?"

"Don't know. They had all night to clean things up. He figures they're long gone."

"So nobody in custody and they're probably still out there. That caller guy, I mean." Meg shook her head.

"Looks like." Dawn stared off into the middle distance and tamped down the feeling of helplessness she'd felt when Wayne had first given her the news. Time to look forward.

"I'm glad you got in to see Timothy. How is he today?"

"Good. He was sitting up, telling stories. Doctor says he'll be home in a few days."

"That's great. I'll go in to see him tonight. He need anything?"

"I asked. He didn't seem to." Meg took a sip of her drink and cocked her head. "How are *you?*"

"You already asked me that."

"Yes, and you asked me. By text. Now I'm asking you face to face." She blinked rapidly. Dawn laughed but she couldn't escape the look of genuine concern in Meg's eyes.

She paused, considering. "I'm bruised but not broken. Busted but not flat."

Meg's brow creased. "Is that from a country song?"

"Too dramatic?"

"It's not from a song?"

Dawn shook her head. "No. The words just popped into my head. Maybe I should write them down."

"Could be the start of a new career," Meg said. "Don't let me interrupt you. You were going to say more."

"It's been a tough few days," Dawn said, turning serious. "But you know what? They can steal my money. They can try to kill my friends. They can trash my boat. But they won't ever take the Papa Joe away from me. And they'll never crush my spirit."

"Now *that* should be a country song." Meg raised her glass. "A toast. To bruised but not broken. Busted but not flat."

Dawn clinked her glass with Meg's and enjoyed the warm feelings flowing through her. She gazed out to sea, content to sit in silence with her friend. Seagulls dipped over a fishing boat coming in late and a small sailboat, much like the Serenity Jane, headed out of the larger marina at the south end of the harbor. Despite her recent troubles, life continued to carry on around her as it always had.

"Hey," Meg said, breaking the silence. "I have a question for you."

"Shoot."

"A few years back, I was a big fan of women's boxing." Meg raised a brow, a non-verbal query. Ah, here was the question Meg had tried to ask her in the speedboat on their way back to the Papa Joe. Dawn resisted the urge to look away and remained quiet. "You're her, aren't you?"

"Who?"

"Come on. I saw how you handled Miguel. And I wasn't there this time, but I know you had to handle him again. You were already beaten and you still came out on top. He's a hell of a big dude."

"Was."

"Are you sure about that?" Meg said.

"No." Dawn thought back to the glimpse of orange life jacket. The turbulent seas, the wall of rain, the thunder and lightning. It was possible he'd pulled a miracle out of his ass and somehow made it to shore. Not likely, but possible. She hated the idea that he might still be walking around somewhere.

"So are you?" Meg tucked a strand of hair behind her ear and stared at Dawn.

"Am I what?"

"Come on, don't be coy. We've been through a lot together." Meg sucked in a breath and watched her. "What's it going to take for you to trust me?"

Dawn met her eyes and tipped her chin, the slightest of movements.

Meg's eyes lit up and she practically bounced in her seat.

"Tropical Storm Dawn. I knew it. I freakin' loved you when you were fighting. You were—" Meg caught the look in Dawn's eyes. She bit her lip then cocked her head to the side again. "I never really understood what happened, I mean, at the end."

"Well that," said Dawn, lifting her glass, "is a story for another day."

———

ALSO BY RILEY CURTS

TROPICAL COAST THRILLER SERIES

NEW DAWN - Dawn Devon - Book 1

GRAY DAWN - Dawn Devon - Book 2

DARK DAWN - Dawn Devon - Book 3
(Available 2022)

9 781777 151584